Crannóg 61 autumn/winter 2024

Editorial Board

Sandra Bunting
Ger Burke
Jarlath Fahy
Tony O'Dwyer

ISSN 1649-4865
ISBN 978-1-907017-71-1

Cover image: *Space Disco Starling* by Graeme Patterson
Cover image sourced by Sandra Bunting
Cover design by Wordsonthestreet
Published by Wordsonthestreet for Crannóg magazine @CrannogM
www.wordsonthestreet.com @wordsstreet

All writing copyrighted to rightful owners in accordance with The Berne Convention

CONTENTS

All in My Head
Aideen Henry 7
Moher
Sean Coffey 12
A Thin Place
Kathleen Magher 17
All that Grows Must be Controlled
Hugo Kelly 23
Judgements and Prophecies
David Lynch 28
Lee's Pool Bar
Aoibheann McCann 33
I Give you my Hand
Katie McIvor 37
Cleanliness is Next to Godliness
Laurence Lumsden 41
Stars
Peter Adair 47
A Note on Place Names
Liam Aungier 48
The Drunken Gardener
Ivy Bannister 49
Inseparable
Gerard Beirne 50
Silent Reading Time
Peter Branson 51
Seers & Mortals
Laura Treacy Bentley 52
Permission
Lauren Camp 54
Peacock in the Car Park
Louise G Cole 56
How to be Bog
Rachael Davey 58
Tolka Cottages
Maurice Devitt 59
A Jigsaw for James Merrill
Maitreyabandhu Dharmachari 60
Some Definitions
Daragh Fleming 61
The History of a Glove
Deborah H. Doolittle 62
Rodent
Maryellen Hodgins 64
Raven's Lullaby
Nicola Geddes 66
Heart of the Fox
Rebecca Gethin 67
Grass
Mark Granier 68

Clonmoylan Summer
   Margaret Hickey 70
A Photo my Blink Took
   Bob Hicok 72
Clear
   Fred Johnston 73
Poems in Search of a Home
   Breda Joyce 74
Fire Alarm
   Claire-Lise Kieffer 76
Official Business
   Brian Kirk 77
Graveyard: Morning
   Robert Leach 78
Seasoning
   Noelle Lynskey 79
On a Christmas Morning
   V.P. Loggins 80
Wet Monday in Galway
   James Martyn Joyce 82
Arguing Into Resistance
   Karen J McDonnell 84
Root
   Kate McHugh 85
Funny Girl
   Alan McMonagle 86
Brine
   Nicole Morris 88
A Hard Night's Work
   John Reinhart 90
Word Cave
   Lorna Shaughnessy 92
The City
   Jo Slade 93
Bring Me Your Hurt
   Breda Spaight 94
How to Let a Wild Thing Go
   Bobbie Sparrow 95
Working in Galway
   Jack Stewart 96
Phillies
   Ling Yuan 98
Will
   Niamh Twomey 100
The Crannóg Questionnaire
   Pete Mullineaux 102
Artist's Statement
   Graeme Patterson 106
Biographical Details 107

Submissions for Crannóg 62 open November 1st until November 30th
Publication date is March 28th 2025

Crannóg is published bi-annually in spring and autumn.

Submission Times:
Month of November for spring issue.
Month of May for autumn issue.

We will <u>not read</u> submissions sent outside these times.

POETRY:
Send no more than three poems. Each poem should be under 50 lines.
PROSE: Send one story. Stories should be under 2,000 words.

We do not accept postal submissions.
When emailing your submission we require three things:
1. *The text of your submission as a Word attachment.*
2. *A brief bio in the third person.*
3. *A postal address for contributor's copy in the event of publication.*

For full submission details, to learn more about Crannóg magazine, to purchase copies of the current issue or take out a subscription, log on to our website:

www.crannogmagazine.com

This issue of Crannóg is dedicated to
the memory of
Fred Johnston
1951 – 2024
Poet, novelist, literary critic, translator, musician

Fred died suddenly in September a few weeks after his poem *Clear* had been accepted for publication in *Crannóg*. The poem appears on page 73.

Suaimhneas síoraí dó

The Crannóg Bursary

The Crannóg Bursary is awarded to one contributor to each issue of *Crannóg*.

When each contributor to *Crannóg* is accepted for inclusion in the magazine they are invited to make a short, simple application for the Crannóg Bursary.

The bursary amounts to €1,500 per issue and the recipient is announced on our social media platforms.

We are grateful to writer Marian Kilcoyne for her sponsorship of the Crannóg Bursary.

All in My Head

Aideen Henry

With me there's before and after.

If you met me before, you'd not notice me in the street, another mammy you'd say to yourself, or not even. Another auld one you might say and that's if you even remembered seeing me. Which you probably wouldn't.

Shoulder length mess of hair with the white ribs lighting up against the black, patchy grey eyebrows, no make-up, faded lips, the pink so pale it's only just visible against the white of my face, and not a piece of jewellery only my wedding ring. I'd be wearing a shapeless dark cardigan over an old t-shirt and stretchy leggings I'd thrown on that morning. The uniform of a busy mother. A flurry of fine white pet hairs over my chest, maybe. The cat, the only one fit to show me any loving.

If you met me on a train and we ended up chatting then I'd tell you about my life, an ordinary life. My husband Tom, a farmer, a good man but a man just the same, my eldest, Kathy, away at college, in her own life now. My two sons Shane and Cian, close to finishing school, and you know boys, in their own world, take no notice of no one. A housewife, I suppose, you could call me. My best friend, Jackie.

I'd had this bad feeling. I'd had it for ages. Thought I was getting depression, coming down with something anyway. I was convinced that something bad was going to happen to me or mine. Not OCD, oh, I'd looked that one up, no rituals, no handwashing, no obsessive cleaning, more's the pity in our house, no locking or checking. It was still there though, hanging in the air around me for weeks like the smell of something gone off.

Jackie was the person I've always been closest to, really. Always. We were best friends at school. First boyfriends together. We even – Lord, when I think of it now – we even had a one night stand with two lads when we were away that weekend together. In the same room. Ah, not sex, like, just kissing and that. We got married around the same time, first babies together. Communions, confirmations, you name it. We even minded each other after our mothers' dying.

And now, I don't know.

You know how there's someone in your life you can say anything to. And I mean anything. That'd be us. I'd know what she was thinking, I'd know when she was hurting about something and not saying. I could read her and she could read me.

Every week we was always doing things together: yoga on Mondays, coffee and cake in her café of a Tuesday, jiving on Thursdays and walking on Saturdays. I wasn't mad about the activities but Jackie was always a live wire, had to be dancing or chasing about and I was happy enough to join her if it meant we were passing the time together. I thought that'd always be the way. That was before.

Now it's after and you wouldn't pass me in the street without taking notice. I'm wearing one of them new smells the young ones do wear. A kind of a mix of flowery, deep heat, peppermint and burning wood if you can imagine such a thing. A sweet burning smell that'd stay with you.

I'm easy on the eye too, a changed woman from before, the grey long gone from my hair, I've it cut short and sharp now and a plum rinse in. My eyebrows is pencilled so I actually have an expression.

Shane says he usen't to know I was annoyed with him about his chores, not done as usual, till he felt the slap on the back of his head. With these new eyebrows, there be less slaps needed all around. The curve of my eyelids is outlined in kohl too, the young one showed me how to put it on, said to me, 'You've lovely almond-shaped eyes, look how they slope down at the sides, that's real unusual.'

And deep red lipstick colours in my lips.

'Definition, that's what you need,' the young one said.

Damn right, says I.

No more stretchy clothes. I wear a jacket cut to fit me, I'm the business now. Tailored trousers, soft leather brogues, an ironed cotton blouse. All the ironing I did in my house over the years and not a thing ironed for myself.

Things was coming to a head. I was right about that.

It was a wet Monday morning and the boys just back at school after mid-term and Jackie and myself were having coffee after yoga. I know, stupid, slow your heart with yoga then set it off at a gallop with coffee.

It was then she told me.

'I've a bit of news for you,' she says. 'I'm moving to Dublin.'

'Jackie, what are you saying?' I said.

'Lookit, I have to go,' she says.

'But, why? What's after happening?'

'I need a change. I can't stick doing the same thing here, over and over,' she says, 'and the exact same people all around me. It's doing my head in.'

'How long for?'

'Oh, months and months. I'm sick of it.'

'How long are you going to Dublin for?'

'A year to start with and then we'll see.'

'How does your hubby feel about it? It'll be a big change for him.'

'He's not coming ... I'm going on my own.'

'Jesus ... well, I can't believe it. If you'd said you were going to the moon it'd be closer.'

'You're overreacting.'

'Me overreacting?' I said. 'That's a fine one coming from you. I'm not the one uprooting my life and hooking it off to Dublin.'

She gave me one of her hard looks. I'd only ever seen her give that look to someone else. Like that day she saw a woman wearing the same shoes she'd just bought herself. Or when a young one passed by with bigger bosoms. That look, it cut to the core.

'Is there a man involved?' I said.

'You think with a husband and four boys I'd be taking on a man too, do you?'

'It's just it's kinda sudden.'

'It's not soon enough, I can tell you.'

'I see.'

'I've been feeling restless this long while, on edge, as though I'm expecting something to happen, hoping for something to change and it's not happening. Expecting the world to bring it to me but sure that's not how it works at all.'

'Oh?'

'If you want something, you have to go after it.'

'And what ... what do you want?'

'I don't rightly know, Liz, but this is not it.'

'I see.'

She lifted her spoon and scraped the foam from around her empty skinny latte cup.

'You'll come visit me? You will, won't you?' she said, licking the spoon, leaving a chocolate line around her mouth that her tongue couldn't reach.

'Will you want me to?'

'Jesus, of course I'll want you to.' She laid down the spoon.

'I don't know,' I said.

I left then, left her sitting there, a ring of chocolate around her mouth I wasn't going telling her about.

I went away in a haze, could make no sense of it.

I said it to Tom the following morning.

'Isn't it well for her,' said Tom.

'You mean you approve?'

'Sure, hasn't she a housekeeper organised to look after her bits of jobs at home for the youngest. Why wouldn't she go if she has a want to?'

'A housekeeper,' I said.

'Mammy,' says Shane, 'you always make too much of things.'

'Where's the lunches?' says Cian.

'In the fridge,' I say, 'and don't forget to take an apple each for after. And use up them old ones before you go opening that new packet.'

Cian forages for an apple and stands there stock still, twisting the stalk, whispering the letters of the alphabet until it snaps off.

It took her three weeks. To organise everything. She'd the job got in Dublin before she told anyone anything. Cute.

It made me look real hard at my own life. No love lost at home for me. A housekeeper, no more. Oh, they love me, no doubt they do, in their way. Tom, Kathy away now and the two boys. But it's all around them. All to suit them. And I, the fool. The fool, no more.

It set me thinking, it did. What I wanted to be doing with myself. With Jackie gone from me, there'd be nothing keeping me at home.

I made my plans.

So, I told them this morning. A sabbatical, I called it.

'A what?' said Cian.

'Every seven years, lecturers up in the college get a year out to do their own thing, to recharge.'

'To recharge,' says Shane.

'Do some research, some reading or writing.'

'Sure, you don't do any reading or writing,' says Shane.

'A year out,' says Tom.

'I'll take six months,' says I.

I'd heard him often enough at the marts bargaining fellas down, than to make the mistake of starting too low.

'Will you be staying here?' says Cian, thinking of his favourite dinners, he was.

'I will in my arse,' says I, 'the home is the workplace of the mammy. I'm going on my travels, no other way to do it.'

'On your travels?' says Shane.

'I'll start in London and see how I go. I've always had a yen for Morocco or maybe Greece. Might be nice to pass the winter there, a bit of heat in my bones.'

'Can we visit you there?' says Shane.

'Little point in me going to Morocco to get away from my family if ye all come trailing after me, expecting me to make dinners for ye.'

'But what about — ' says Tom.

'Oh, I've Carmel all organised to do my bits and pieces. She's not too dear either. I've a bit put aside that'll get me over there. And sure, won't they pay me to work, wherever I go?'

'They'll pay you for housework?' says Shane.

'Will you not be lonely?' says Cian, the small boy not altogether gone out of my baby.

'Sure, amn't I lonely here and ye gone all day at school, then at hurling or football and jobs waiting for me at every turn in this house that has me sick to death of cleaning it and that forever looks dirty no matter what. Anyway, I'll be too busy to be lonely. And can't I ring ye if I am and hear all your news.'

Well, they don't like it much, I can tell you. But that's the way it is now. I'll be going on my travels next Sunday.

As for Jackie, she got a bit of a land.

'You're leaving ... the country?'

'I am,' I said.

'But I won't see you.'

'You won't. But sure, you wouldn't anyway and you up in Dublin.'

She looked disappointed. As though I'd beaten her to it. I hadn't thought of it like that.

She told me how she didn't think I'd have the nerve to pull it off. Funny that. I don't know if that girl knows me at all.

And the high regard I had for her always.

All in my head.

Moher

Sean Coffey

Dread. The dank dark fields, the grey roiling ocean, the sinew of road winding upwards, the skittering rain. The heights glimpsed behind shrouds of mist trailed by vagrant clouds. An unquiet landscape, the light altogether wrong, and always there in his childhood imagination, the cliffs, their awful fall, the depths. The dread. Moher. He turned away, surveyed the windswept pier, the battered Portakabin used by the ferry companies. A chalk-board in a window read 'Time of Next Sailing'. Underneath was scrawled 'March', as if days, hours, and minutes had lost their currency. Which was fitting.

After walking back to the car, he sat in, straightened the seat-back and pulled the door shut. The windows were fogged with his night's breath so he started the engine and set the blower on to clear them. Reaching for his bottle of water he discovered it fallen sideways, half its contents drained into the passenger seat. No one to sit there now. Taking up the bottle, he drained the remains into himself.

His shoes were destroyed, witness to his last night's failure. Feet clammy in damp socks, he reached forward and diverted the engine blast to warm them. The darkness hadn't been dark enough, the whiskey fog not dense enough. He'd got to the edge but the blind step into the abyss was too much and he'd withdrawn, muddied and beaten.

He reached down to the torn carton at his feet, extracted the sandwich that remained and chewed on it mechanically. Brute fuelling, no savour to anything, now. There would just have to be another way. He lay back on the seat and became drowsy in the warmth, lulled by the purr of the fan. A rehearsal, maybe, for the hose-pipe, the rolled scarf sealing the gap, the death-doze. Content with this, he fell into a sleep.

He woke with a start some time later. It took a heart-stopping moment for him to place himself, but then the frightful events of the previous afternoon exploded into his mind in graphic detail. He recoiled horrified at what he'd done, grief and self-pity driving him back to the edge. But now when he looked it was a sea of rage he saw, in all its violence and drama. Without hesitation he let himself fall into it. If he was going to hell, then by Christ he wasn't going alone.

Back up the hill, back past the cliffs, still dreadful but triumphal now too, jeering him for his cowardice. A turning to the left, a road between folds of a hill, a laneway, grass-grown in the middle. A yellow-painted farmhouse, single-storey, plasterwork ornamentations neatly picked out in pink. Dormant sheds long retired but still dignified in their Liscannor slab caps. Everything just so. Everything as it ever was.

She was slow to answer his ring, his grandmother, his father's mother, his granny. Granny, when he came to stay in the summer to spend time with his sisters. Granny, when he said goodbye in late August to go back to his mother's people in far-away Limerick. And the cousins who were his family.

'Hah. You've come,' she crowed on opening the door. His sisters had told her of the break-up, hardly a surprise. He followed her into the kitchen, high wooded ceilings and two-tone walls, lime below and cream above, oil-cloth on the table, patterned. Loud tick of wall-clock. Everything just so. Everything as it ever was.

Except her, the face grown smaller, her grip on the kettle grown weaker. Struggling now to enact her loveless tea ceremony.

'I suppose she'll get the house,' she said to the milk jug, then set it on the table pointing at him. Without waiting for a response she went back to the worktop and began sawing at a loaf of her famous soda bread. But with some difficulty. 'I knew she was bad news, that one,' she went on, as a slice fell away, a misshapen, broken wedge. 'No better than she should be,' she muttered and began sawing again.

'Cathy,' he named his wife for her, sharp, like a knife-strike. But her leathery, stale-crust skin turned the thrust aside. She merely gave a grunt and completed birthing a second mutant slice out of the heel.

'Is there another man?' she said, plating up the bread. 'I suppose there is, a strap like that,' she mused when he didn't respond. He watched her approach the table, reach to lay the plate down only to have it escape her arthritic fingers and clatter derisively onto the oilcloth. Clever plate – more robust than she was, it would outlast her, and they all knew it. He returned the spilled slices to its willow-pattern solidity and got to his feet. He couldn't be watching her.

He fetched over cups and saucers, the Flora she called butter, the shop-bought jam, a knife or two. The steaming kettle clicked itself off and though she reached for it he was faster. For a moment both their hands met on its plastic handle, then he jerked it away, turning his back on her to begin scalding the pot. She withdrew to sit at the table.

'You men,' she muttered. 'Your father was the same. Soft.' The teapot filled, he took it up and moved to the table. Taking care not to bring it crashing down on her skull, he placed it on a table mat, then sat himself. 'Coming crying to me about your mother,' she went on, 'how he wasn't able for her.'

'Is that why you sent me away? In case I'd turn out like him?'

'No. It was your mother's people who insisted you come to them.'

'Was it?' he muttered, poured their tea and dribbled in some milk. 'I suppose they thought one murderer in the family was enough,' he said and brought his cup to lip. Seen across an infinity pool of tea, his grandmother began to dwindle, growing smaller and more distant in time. All his life he'd wanted to say 'murder'. Now he'd done it.

She began smathering Flora onto one of the slices. No plate, crumbs scattering all across the oilcloth. Then the jam, a big child's dollop scooped out and smeared across bread and oilcloth without distinction. He watched, fascinated, as she grabbed up the mess and pressed it to her face, her jaw already working in anticipation. Vacant hollow eyes as she gobbled it down in greedy gulps, then employed her sleeve as a napkin, drawing it witlessly across her jaw from crook to cuff. As a snotty child might do. He was six when it happened. Six when they were all separated. Six when the devil came to visit.

'Oh she was bad news, that one,' she said, then sucked vehemently at her cup and took a swallow. From the downturn of her lips on each side, two glistening moisture trails formed, striking southwards for her chin.

'Who, Granny? Who was bad news? My mother? Or Cathy?' She gazed at him bleary-eyed and unseeing. Was it an act, a ruse, this sudden confusion, this sudden regression? Or had her endless disseminating finally caught up with her? Tricked her out of herself, just as she'd tricked him out of himself.

'Sure I know you didn't mean to hurt her, sweetie.' Out of nothing tears had pooled in her muddied eyes, a second pair of rivulets begun to course down her face.

'It's me, Granny. Shane, not my da,' he said sharply. 'Shane, not Paudie,' he added, but with less conviction. She gazed at him.

'Ah Paudie,' she murmured and sniffled.

He leapt to his feet in a rage. So this was it, her last, most spiteful act of all – to unmake him completely. To totally expunge him.

'You malignant old bitch!' he loomed over her and raised a clenched fist. She didn't stir, or cower, or make any reaction. If anything, she seemed to be waiting, suddenly so still, so rapt. She knew. She understood. He relaxed his hand, let his arm fall to his side and straightened up. He wouldn't do her the favour. He wouldn't deliver her. Turning away, he walked to the door and without looking back continued on out of the house, got into his car and set it moving.

Feeling nothing, he navigated back out to the main road. But when he got to the junction he had to stop because he no longer had a way to go. The part of him who did was still back at the house, could probably never leave it. Confounded, he sat until a car beeped and he had to choose a direction. So he did, turning left towards Lahinch.

The road was quiet, no sightseers or coaches this grey January day. A squad-car passed going the other direction, but then some miles later it was in his rear-view mirror, following behind. His heart suddenly leapt to his mouth. Could the alarm be raised already? A layby presented itself, he indicated and swerved into it precipitately, braking hard in a spray of chippings. The squad-car went on by, continuing down the hill without stopping. He leant forward, rested his brow on the steering wheel. What was he to do? His resolve was all gone. Suddenly he was terrified, in a cold sweat, coming asunder. Panic rising, he pushed the door open, climbed out and turned to stand, his arms outspread across its roof. Breathing deeply, he gazed out over the landscape. Below and to the right, the low jumbled buildings of Liscannor, beyond them a blue finger of ocean pointing into Lahinch. He knew exactly where he was now, and when he turned, there was the grotto of St. Brigid's Well burrowed into the hillside, above it the trees an archway for the steps up to the graveyard.

Pain stabbed at his heart. He'd brought Cathy here the first time they'd come together to Moher. How she'd wondered at its paganness, at the homespun idolatry of its statues, ribbons and photos. He'd been quiet, then, so dark a place and him being so dark himself. But now he knew he must face it. Crossing over the road he entered the dim cavern, heard the tinkling trickle of the water from the rockface. The eyes of the innumerable dead gazed out at him from photographs, neither accusatorial nor forgiving, neither curious nor uncaring. Cathy was with them now, he'd sent her to join them. The pool of grief inside him began to overspill, its waters rising, closing over his head, and he began to drown. Yet all the while was the gentle trickle of the water from the rockface. And the certainty that he was no longer alone.

Back outside, stone steps to the graveyard beckoned him upwards. When they forked into two separate curving flights, he took the left one. He found he wasn't alone, and greeted an old man who was carefully descending the leaf-slicked stone. On the other flight, an old woman was struggling to ascend. When he got to the top, the graveyard fanned out before him across the hillside. But he turned to look back at the couple doing their stations. The woman was frail, and he worried for her on the so-steep incline.

They said his mother had fallen down the stairs. A terrible accident. But he knew better, six years old though he was. And how the campaign was begun, that she'd been drinking, that she'd been seen to fall before. How her drunkard husband, his guilty father, had subsequently fallen into the grave after her. And how he too had now fallen in his turn.

Beginning the descent himself, he passed the old woman, slowing so that he stayed just below her, able to catch her if she fell. At the bottom, she gave him a faint, grave smile, then continued on for the next round. He crossed the road, got back into his car, and after a time, began the journey to hand himself in.

A Thin Place

Kathleen Magher

Rae hears that very annoying sound of a car alarm, that incessant honking, and the dull ding-dinging of the doorbell. Her eyes bolt open from sleep, eyelids slightly sticking to her eyeballs; she rubs them out gently and the first thing she sees are those fingerprints on the ceiling.

'Fingerprints, car alarms, door bells. All this in the country,' Rae mutters. 'It's supposed to be quiet here, but that's never been true unless you're on a farm.'

She takes another look at the fingerprints.

'Must have been the time I got you to change the light fixture,' she says to an empty room. 'It's the one thing I don't miss about you. Your damn fingerprints all over the place. Me always wiping up after you, and you telling me your hands were clean whenever I'd mention it.'

She grabs an oversized plaid shirt and pulls it on over her t-shirt and flannel bottoms, struggling with the buttons. 'People are patient here though,' Rae says out loud, quickly getting a look at herself in the dresser mirror, pulling back her dishevelled hair turned true white. She gathers it into a thin pony, before doing ...

'What next?'

Ding ding.

'Oh yes, the damn doorbell. Someone is at the door.'

Rae's ancestral home is not like the other houses in the village, it being English Victorian rather than French Canadian. Built in 1891, the house features a set of bay windows on either side of the front doors on both first and second floors, with two thirds of it enclosed by a wrap-around windowed porch covered with cedar shakes. All of it inspires immensity. People like to look at it; admire it and how the window casings are all still original wood that have been painted summers upon summers – white upon green upon brown – keep it white, that's easiest, and the maintenance of it all to keep its beauty alive. Still, it will never be perfect. There is always something off about it – cracked windows, broken cedar shingles, rotted sills, peeling paint, split steps, and now the upper railing is needing replacement. It's hard to keep up, especially since Joe passed away ten years ago, in the year 2020.

Rae is on her way down the flight of stairs, twelve steps recently renewed to their former glory. They no longer creak or send slicing splinters into the soles of her feet; now they feel great to step upon in bare feet.

Who's at the door? Two men dressed in suits. Never a good sign, Rae muses as she opens the door.

'*Bonjour madame.*' They both smile, revealing nice white teeth. '*Désolé de vous déranger madame.* You speak French?'

'*Oui, et vous êtes?*'

'I am Jean-François Cloutier. My assistant, Maurice Roy.'

Rae sighs heavily. It's always been this way. Her accent has the undesired effect of making any native French speaker switch to English, or the desired effect of being told, *vous avez un bel accent.*

'*Vous êtes Irlandaise?*'

'What's this about?' Rae, tight-lipped, holding in her annoyance.

'May we enter?'

'*Oui, bien sûr.*' Rae beckons them in. Yes, I'm Irish, *native de Frampton.* What can I do for you?'

'We are from the *Ministère des Nouvelles Technologies.* Last month, we receive a complaint that there are problems with car alarms engaging, and clients of the bistro not able to use their *clé fob* and not able to get back into their cars.'

'Did the bistro make the complaint?' Rae says, her head pointing to the next-door neighbour.

'Yes, madame. Are you the *propriétaire* of this house?'

Rae nods her head, her lips firmly together. Can't they see, she has been the owner of the house for a long time now.

'We have determine that there is interference signal coming from the *proximité* of your house, *madame.* May we inspect and make some tests?'

'Tests? What kind of tests and may I see some ID?'

They ask her if she has internet and if there have been any problems.

No problems.

They ask her if she has a microwave oven, a cordless phone, Bluetooth, a video camera, a cell phone or any fluorescent lights. No to all of it.

The two young men get out their electronic hand-held data pad devices and they begin in the basement, pointing it here and there, across the cords of wood and along the stone ledge covered with insulating foam. Then they stick their device up the cavity of the large *Legaré* wood furnace, the house's main heating system. But it's all about vents and flues, dampers and fire. Nothing about it is digital or electronic. They go on to remove the chimney clean-out plate and check there, holding the device inside and up the brick chimney towards the open sky, searching for a reading of something.

Upstairs now, to read the kitchen and first floor. Then to the second floor. Four bedrooms and one tiny bathroom. Not one technological item up there. It's all old. They ask her where the attic is. She points to a small square removable section of the ceiling and she gets them a stepladder and they peer through. Not wanting to crawl through in their suits (plus they already have soot on their sleeves from the chimney inspection test), the assistant Maurice shoots his electronic hand-held device at arm's length in every direction of Rae's attic.

Back downstairs now, and Rae slips on her shoes. Out the back door, through the mudroom to the summer-kitchen. They both comment on the pristine pink *Bélanger* wood cook stove that's there, then they walk through the adjoining shed, which mostly contains gardening tools, rakes and hoes and broken-handled shovels. No modern-day technology out there either.

Outside now. Sixty feet by sixty feet of property. They aim their hand-held machines in every direction of Rae's yard. They peer up the massive galvanised angle-iron television tower that Rae's father had installed back in the day when signals were sought after this way. But now it's just a massive tower, doing nothing. No matter, they aim their hand-held devices upwards towards the tower searching for some latent something.

Next, they check Rae's car and ask to see her car opener.

'*C'est simple.*' Rae shows them the key. Joe's 1991 Toyota Corolla still runs, and Rae can see them both admiring the car, smiling like it's a showpiece.

After all their inspections are done, the gentlemen from the *Ministère des*

Nouvelles Technologies and Rae return to her enclosed front porch. They tell her they need her signature, and they hand her their device and she holds her pointer finger steady with her middle finger and thumb, her finger becoming a pencil now, and scrawls her name on the screen.

After all is said and done, they tell her that they can find no interference signal.

Damn car alarm still at it.

'A report will be sent to the *municipalité. Et votre maison, madame,* your house, she has *une âme, on la sent.*'

'A soul, yes,' Rae repeats. 'Many people sense it. *Merci.*'

'*C'est moi qui vous remercie.*' And they are gone.

Rae, down on her knees now, removes the cover to her well and whispers, 'How in hell they overlooked shooting their devices down here I don't know. Must've been your car that distracted them.'

The well was divined in the year 1900, a step towards modern times. No longer necessary to go to the public well when you have the water right below you – in Rae's case right under the front porch of her house. Everyone knew that this particular well water was superb and still is and it comes out of Rae's tap, the only household in the village still on well-water. Over the years, they warned her about it. She could get sick and die from drinking contaminated well-water. She should get hooked up to the town's treated water. They sent her warnings and waivers and whatnot, stuff she kept ignoring. Then they decided they should test her water and inspect her well in the spirit of concern for her health. They do so once a year now without fail.

If they could only get rid of the interference signal, they'd be ready to go with the long-awaited cell phone tower that would bring reliable service.

'That's what all the fuss is about, Joe. They want to get on with development.'

She gets dressed and heads over to the post office to check her box. There is a letter from the municipality asking for a *suivi*. A follow-up.

The mayor, frustrated over the lack of cell phone service, is putting it out to the people now to write to the government. He has a package all prepared. It contains a letter with his signature, a motion with twenty-one reasons why the government should do something about the lack of cell phone service in the municipality, with a space for a signature, and a map of Frampton. All to be included in the stamped addressed envelope.

Rae throws the whole thing in the recycling bin.

'It will never work. Thin place here. And not just here. Other places too. Cripes, you can go on guided tours of the thin places in Ireland. Now that is something I would have liked to do.'

She pours herself a glass of water.

'Not just that, she continues. 'The Irish did the research. Last year, they found out that interference signals common to all those places made cell phoning a useless endeavour. That's what they found out,' Rae's voice trailing off as she raises her glass to no one at all.

That evening is the council meeting, the one where they have Rae's well as an agenda item again. They wish to decommission it. To do that they need to plug it up and the easiest way is through Rae's access point on her porch. This time they have all the paperwork from the various ministries and offices throughout the province, all officially stamped and duly signed. Yet all the paperwork and permissions and mandates and orders are for naught.

'Rae has what is called an acquired right to her well.' M. Paul Bonneau rises as he speaks.

He is at the meeting. Rae is grateful for his presence. Her notary. He knows all the ins and outs of her house deed. Nice of him to come.

'*Merci*, Paul.'

'They may take it to court, Rae. At some point, it might require that you get a lawyer,' Paul tells her as he walks her out of the meeting. 'Would you like a ride home?'

'No thank you, Paul. I like to walk.'

Rae walking home now, slowly. Breathing in the night air. Fall. Crisp. Leaves crunching under her feet. Coyotes in the hills, yipping and howling and barking, warning others not to cross their territorial boundaries. She takes in long deep breaths, feels panic rising in her chest or is it anger? The first thing she does when she steps onto her porch is she pulls the metal handle of her well and gets down on her hands and knees and peers into its depths.

'Are you there, Joe? I need help. Ya hear?' Rae shouts into the porch floor hatch. 'They're coming for the well. The interference signal is what they're after.'

Rae pauses, looks to see that no one is walking by. An old woman on her hands and knees, talking to herself.

That evening Rae lies awake in bed, staring at Joe's fingerprints.

It was a month or so later that the *Ministère de l'Eau Potable*, the drinking-water ministry agents came by for their annual inspection of Rae's well and testing of her water.

They pulled at the metal handle, but nothing. The cover didn't budge.

'*Madame*, it's as if it is locked from the inside. Sealed? How is this possible?'

And that's when Rae saw them. Unmistakable. Joe's fingerprints all over the cover, keeping it in place, holding things down.

All that Grows Must be Controlled

Hugo Kelly

Mrs Philips was perplexed about the baby. When or where this little baby existed was a matter of confusion but nevertheless, she remembered distinctly the child's fluttering hands and pudgy thighs and that it reeked of life like a little squealing animal. It was a boy. She was sure of that but, try as she could, no more information would come to mind. It was very frustrating.

She sighed to herself now and adjusted her dressing gown so that it covered her knees and looked out at the gathering evening. The air was still warm, and the sky was tinted a soft yellow by the lowering sun. Just beyond the overgrown lawn of the Atlantic Pilgrim Nursing home, the nearby river had thinned to little more than a stream. The best summer in years she thought, a little bitterly. Well, she wanted none of it. Far in the distance a grey sheen of smoke was visible on the horizon. The whin bushes had been set alight by accident or design and whole tracts of the far-off hills were smouldering. More reasons to distrust summer she thought. All that grows must be controlled. That was the truth.

On her left, hidden by the opened door, Kris-with-a-K was finishing one of his strong-smelling cigarettes. He was a strapping Polish lad, with wide shoulders that blossomed into a powerful neck and head. She wondered what he was thinking as he stared out at the pleasant scene. Did he miss home? Or his family? Perhaps he was glad to be away from them.

Maria, one of the nurses from the Philippines, said that he was terrified of heights and couldn't work on building sites. Poor Kris-with-a-K she thought spending his time lifting the elderly residents of the Atlantic Pilgrim Nursing Home instead of the hods of mortar that he was surely built for. He had poor English, and his most common phrase was a softly blasphemous *Hesuz Kryzt, Hesuz Kryzt* which he used with different tones and inclinations to deal with any situation. If she had an accident or fell out of bed he would appear hissing 'HEZUS KRYZT HEZUS KRYST!' But if she passed him a twenty euro note he would smile and purr 'Hesuzz Kryyzzzt, Hesuzz Kryyyzzzt' in deep gratitude.

He now finished his cigarette and pushed it into the dusty clay at his feet. He looked anxiously back into the corridor of the home searching, she guessed, for Chris-with-a-C, the General Manager of the home who flowed about the premises like a spilt bottle of milk. Judging that the coast was clear, Kris-with-a-K lifted one finger to indicate that he would return in one hour to bring her back in. Mrs Philips nodded and made a thumbs up sign, glad to be on her own at last. It was time to think about the baby again.

She had risked mentioning the child to a few people but that had not been a sensible move. Her nephew Thomas and his wife Geraldine looked at her askance when she brought up the baby at their visit earlier in the day.

'You must be a little tired, Margaret.' Thomas said. 'There's no baby. Uncle Matt and yourself didn't have any children.'

'What?' she said. 'That doesn't make any sense. There was a little baby. I'm sure of it. It was a greasy brown colour and cried like a lamb.'

'You're watching too much television,' Geraldine said. 'I think that was a plot line on *Fair City*.'

'I don't watch *Fair City*,' Mrs Philips had replied tersely.

'It might have been on *Emmerdale* then,' Geraldine said.

Mrs Philips had felt her anger and frustration grow. It was best not to say anything more about the baby she decided. That evening she asked Kris-with-a-K to wheel her from her room to the very back of the home. There he opened the emergency exit and pushed her out into the air. Here she could look towards the river and the tall ivy-covered trees that rustled with magpies and the attentions of the summer breeze. It was here that she could think in peace about the baby.

At first nothing about the child would come back to her at all. She had been a young woman living at home on the crest of adulthood. Her parents were gentle but remote people. Her mother prayed and baked. Her father had worked and smoked. This was the family way. There was a secretarial school nearby where she learned shorthand and typing, preparing for her life ahead. She wore bright blue dresses and people for the first time noticed her. That fact seemed important. And yet, despite these recollections of youthful times, she knew that there was something missing.

Her eyes fell on the thick green trees in the distance just beyond the river. They seemed very familiar. Yes, she thought something had definitely happened underneath a canopy of trees. If I go back to those trees she thought, perhaps I will remember more about the baby.

She sat back gathering her strength and then unsteadily stood up. She did feel a little dizzy and yet there was a sense of intense delight that at long last she was going to get to the bottom of this mystery. She took a faltering step forward and then another one across the soft lawn. When she came to the fence she could see the thin panels were collapsed and rotten and delightfully she pulled back the thin wood that ripped like paper to make a gap that she could walk though. All of a sudden she felt nervous and unsure of herself. But still she continued on, looking towards the trees and their long drooping branches that reached out to her.

She paused at the river's edge. There was very little water, just a trickle sliding over the short ledge of a waterfall onto the black riverbed that shone like marble in the half light. There seemed no choice if she wanted to reach the trees. And so, she stepped into the river, taking small careful steps that barely seemed to disturb the water. But then the depth increased ever so slightly and the cold water spilled into her light shoes. Awkwardly she took another step, her foot lodging between two barely submerged stones. She tottered and lost her balance, falling backwards and landing on the ledge of the waterfall in a sitting position as the beer-coloured water slid around her.

'Oh,' she said too surprised to feel any discomfort.

The water, faintly warmed by the heat of the day, flowed around her waist and trickled down her legs. The shock threw all her confused thoughts and memories into the air. And finally they fell in a sequence that she could at last understand.

It had happened just beyond her house along the Lane in the middle of the night. She had been too frightened to wake anyone and when the pain became too much she had tottered out of the house, down the dark boreen. It had been July then too with the air warm and thick with nature's breath. She had lain down underneath the tall birch trees.

The ground had been dry and there had been the tongue-shaped leaves of cowslips clustering everywhere. The pain had been unbearable, worse was the loneliness. She had felt so forsaken. And perhaps she had been. But as is the way nature had carried on bitterly indifferent to her plight. The labour continued and a little boy had been born. The boy cried and she tried to comfort him. Perhaps it was the crying that brought her family, but she had been found and taken back to her house. Her mother had looked after her through clenched teeth. Her father remained silent, unable it seemed to find words. In fact all the words had been left to the family doctor.

'The father?' he had asked her simply.

'He went to Australia,' she said. 'He fixes typewriters. I wrote to him but didn't hear back.'

'I see,' the doctor said.

'He's not a bad man,' she had said pathetically as if trying to defend herself by defending him.

'But he's not a good one either,' the doctor replied with grim assurance.

The doctor packed away his stethoscope.

'You are young,' he said. 'You are strong. Your life is ahead of you. This does not need to hold you back. Do you follow me?'

She had nodded, taking comfort in his assured manner. But still at the time she did not understand what this pronouncement meant. She must have been in a type of shock because a series of confused days passed. And then one day when she felt better she realised that the baby was gone. The boy had been given up for adoption. It was all for the best everyone agreed.

She thought about that for a while as she sat there in the water. The sensation in her heart was raw, almost bitter. She had married a few years later but no children had come. And somehow she had managed to put aside the memory of the thrashing infant lying on the bed of dried leaves and ferns. She supposed she had done that just so she could survive.

But now as the darkness fell she gripped her thin hand into a fist.

'I was right,' she said. 'There was a baby.'

Above her a soft darkness had smudged the sky and a full moon was glowing dim in the early evening. Its rays reflected off the thin water, shining like silver all around her. She thought again about the boy lying at her feet. She wished she had given him a name. She reached her hand down into the moon's reflection on the water and lifted a silvery handful in her palm. 'I name you Paul,' she said and spilt the water back into the river.

The boy, she realised, was now an older man, perhaps also out on this summer evening with the same bright moon shining down on him. She hoped that he was happy. The water flowed gently about her. The moon moved in and out of clouds. The water glistened, faded, and then brightened like a smile again.

Then she heard excited steps coming in her direction.

A tall figure was running through the thick undergrowth. The shadow stopped at the river's edge, and she could hear heavy breathing. The figure clutched his head with both hands in apparent panic.

'Oh HHHESSUZZ KRRRIZTTT! Oh HHHESSUZZ KRRRIZTTT!'

Kris-with-a-K had come for her.

'I'm quite all right,' she mumbled though her voice sounded weak and she suddenly felt cold. Kris-with-a-K strode into the river and without a pause he reached down and lifted her fully up in his thick arms, cradling her, so that for a moment she felt like a matinee heroine in the Ritz cinema that she had frequented as a girl.

'I was right. There was a baby,' she said smugly.

But Kris-with-a-K did not respond as he stepped onto the river-bank and into the reach of the warm glow of the lights from the home. Instead he groaned to himself deeply and then let out a loud baleful sigh.

Hezuss.....Kkkkkrrrrrizzzzt.'

'Well, I'm sorry if I'm a burden,' Mrs Philips said but, thinking again, thanked him for his help. He mumbled something incoherent and she closed her eyes, enjoying the sensation of being carried. Now as they made their way back through the garden she opened her eyes and looked up. The ink blue sky was dotted with faint stars. She could not remember the last time she had noticed them. Very nice she thought. Very nice indeed.

Judgements and Prophecies

David Lynch

You've got to wonder what the purpose of prophecy is, if you just go ahead and ignore it.

My mother *had* warned me.

It was during those final months of lucidity, her mind still lingering in the narrowing clearing, before it began its long slog, out into the dense woodland of confusion.

'Joe's a nice lad,' she said, 'but there's not much to him. You get me, Claire? Not enough to keep someone like you occupied.'

My mother had only met Joe a few times by then, but she was always at that sort of thing – delivering sweeping pronouncements regarding the substance of people. There was 'nothing much' to that one, 'not a lot going on' in the other. This judgemental side faded, around the same time she began mixing me up with her sister.

But why *did* I fall for Joe?

The thing is, I was led to believe he was smart, and I fancied smart. Yeah, I know, I can't actually be all that smart myself if I was fooled.

In my defence, a number of things fuelled my naiveté.

One major influence was overhearing the few aul' lads, who hung over the pitch-side railing, as they watched Joe play left-corner forward for the club.

I'm the oldest of three girls. None of us all that sporty. So despite not giving one fig about hurling, I'd trod down to matches by my father's side.

Those aul' lads who stood near us were always going on about how Joe was such an 'intelligent player'. How he knew when 'to pick the perfect pass'.

How it required 'brains' to realise when best 'to drop the shoulder, ghost past a defender and stick one over the bar', or when to choose 'stepping inside to hand-pass if off'.

'That Joe Harrington is a very smart player,' my father declared more than once at home. He delivered this judgement loudly, and unprompted, as if he was the oracular receptor of the universe's intention to inform me that Joe Harrington was brainy.

Then one drizzly Tuesday afternoon, I was standing in the newsagent on Market Lane. There on the *Champion*'s front page, tucked underneath a story about a burst water mains outside the town's post-office, was a small photo of Joe swinging his hurl. His picture was nestled above a narrow strapline that declared:

Joe Harrington smartly picks his points to ensure victory

I honour print, even if it's just the *Champion*.

So the local media, the aul' lads at the club and the universe through my Delphic father had collectively concluded that Joe was Einstein with a hurl, Camus in studs.

Actually, that comparison is not so fanciful. Camus did regularly pull on a pair of boots as a young soccer goalkeeper in Algeria.

I love Camus. Cool, smart, smoking hot.

Joe was no Camus, but he was grand-looking in a rock solid sort of way. In the *Champion*'s photo he was smiling. It was a nice smile. As far as things went in this town, he was on the positive side of okay in the looks department.

The Leaving was five years past, I had deferred college after my mother began showing early signs. My father urged me to go, but I knew he needed me about.

So ... Jesus this is embarrassing to recall, this was before Tinder and stuff. It was before girls could go straight up and ask a lad out. Although I'm not sure if that's even really a thing now? Anyway, I began positioning myself within Joe's outer orbit. In O'Brien's on a Saturday night I would sit at a table with my friend Tess, and when I went to the toilet I'd angle my route so I'd pass close to where Joe usually sat up at the counter.

But nothing much happened. The odd time he nodded at me. He blushed. That was another generator of attraction. His reticence. I imagined his mind as a vast swirling reservoir. I often laid down in bed, conjuring up what Joe must be thinking right at that moment. I never focused on any specific detail, I just fell back and drenched myself in the dark churning waters of his silent intellect. I was convinced something was going on in there, hidden beneath his hurling helmet, something big and powerful and saturating. It made me wet.

Then one Saturday in O'Brien's, Joe approached me and in a low voice asked what I was drinking. He was polite, his cheeks seared crimson from the heat of the bar and his shyness. It was cute.

He sat down at our table, but as the evening progressed he said very little. Lads constantly came up to him, laughing and exchanging senseless drunken statements. He did not flinch on impact from the numerous friendly palms slammed upon his back. There was a constant whirlwind of action around the town's star hurler. But Joe was the calm epicentre of it all, sitting there smiling and quiet. Thinking.

But now I know he wasn't. *Thinking*, that is.

As those initial weeks built into months, in O'Brien's and elsewhere, Joe remained rather muted, while I became increasingly intrigued.

Now when I interrogate my memory, it's embarrassingly apparent that during that dizzy cyclone of raucous male banter, those endless laughs and jokes in O'Brien's, Joe hardly participated. His teammates were in awe of his talent, so he got a pass on not being fascinating, or entertaining, or smart, or funny. He got a pass on having to say or contribute anything of interest at all.

But somehow, this remained largely invisible to me as our relationship began and developed. Maybe it was the rapid amassing of life's clutter that distracted me from the truth. Work, weekends away, renting the apartment together, the comically early wedding, the grinding routine as my mother's chief carer.

But there are moments planted in my mind. Signposts, that, on reflection, pointed in the direction of a town called 'dopey'.

Examples?

I feel bad recalling them.

Okay, right so, just two.

I stopped going to mass pretty early in my teens despite my parents' moaning. I'm an atheist, not because of some dramatic conversion, I just stopped believing. Simple as that. Don't get me wrong, I respect Jesus and his message, I'm a fan of his life story actually, even the miracles. Basically, I'm on board until the resurrection. That's the Hollywood-twist that lost me.

But Joe never missed mass.

So, it was some banal Sunday morning, Joe was rinsing his cereal bowl before he got ready to walk to 10 a.m. service. I was sitting at his parents' kitchen table, staring into my coffee mug. I looked up towards the back of his head.

'Joe, do you really believe in God? Like, up in heaven, with a big beard sitting on his throne?'

He turned to me. 'Yes,' he said, then turned back to the sink and started to dry his bowl.

My eyes watered. I nearly cried because I pitied the crystalline assuredness of his answer, the astonishing purity of his elementary faith.

Look, don't get me wrong, people have their beliefs, and I'm not one to totally deny that something may be out there. I've even dipped into a bit of quantum physics and other crazy stuff. I'm aware that I don't know much. But it was the simple-mindedness of the response that floored me. Joe, the grown adult I'd judged to go out with.

The second example? Another ordinary weekend was winding down a year or so later. He was sitting watching *The Sunday Game*. I was at the other end of our sofa slowly working my way through *Midnight's Children*.

Out of nowhere he began speaking out loud towards the TV.

'During a match, you must step forward. Create facts, rather than expect things to happen. Seize it.'

I put the book down. I looked up at the TV, half expecting to see those words appear on the screen, with my new husband reading them aloud like a zombie. But the highlights of the Cork–Tipp Munster final were still on.

So my mind concentrated on his words, picking them up and carefully turning them over, gazing on each with wonder. This sounded like the basic building blocks of a personal philosophy. Look, I'm not saying his observations were outtakes from Kant or Plato's greatest hits, or anything like that. But by Joe's standards, they were not bad at all. It was simply the most interesting thing I'd ever heard him say. And what was more outstanding, he wasn't finished yet.

'*You* must be the change in the game,' he continued, eyes still on the screen. 'Don't allow the game just happen to you. Don't let the high winds throw you off course. You must *be* the wind.'

I smiled and allowed a few seconds of silence to breathe, fearful that any careless interjection could prematurely end my husband's impromptu sermon on the sofa. This was perhaps a glimpse into the Joe I felt I'd been promised by the aul' lads at the pitch-side, by my father, by the *Champion*'s sub-editor.

Eventually, when it became apparent further nuggets of insight weren't forthcoming, I raised my voice, hoping to nudge our relationship someplace new and compelling.

'A bit like life, Joe, don't you think?'

He looked at me, smiled, then shook his head gently as if what I'd said was the most ridiculous thing ever to be uttered in all of Christendom.

'What do you mean?' he asked, still smiling.

I went to answer, but before I could, he added, 'That's crazy talk, Claire.'

There was a painful ache in my stomach, a contraction caused by evacuating hope. I sighed and reopened my book.

A quarter of an hour later as *The Sunday Game* credits rolled, he smiled and whispered, 'Like life,' while shaking his head again.

I could no longer spin it to myself. The truth was I married a dope. A loving and loyal husband, but a dope. I hate saying that. I know it's mean. It's open to obvious retorts, like 'Sure you were the real idiot to marry him, weren't you?'

But what can I say? It's the bald truth of it.

He's actually a better person than me in many ways. His calmness is lovely. He's a really good fella. But I just wanted someone to discuss things with, things that went beyond what we're having for dinner, or the latest results in the championship.

But who am I to be so judgemental?

It's my fault.

My mother *had* warned me.

One thing I understand now is that the early part of a relationship resembles an ardent cult, with its wild prophecies of a happy future, the blind faith, its suspension of judgement. Its trances. Its lies. But after some time, a relationship becomes less like a cult, and more like traditional religion, orthodox and full of unconscious ritual. It's at that moment some of us begin to question our faith.

I asked for a divorce three weeks after my mother entered the nursing home.

Joe sighed. 'I could've predicted this,' he said.

Lee's Pool Bar

Aoibheann McCann

If you are hot and tired and can't walk any further, if you squint at the faded writing on the sandwich board and decide that yes, you could do with a cold poolside beer just follow the chalk arrow down the alley between the apartments and you will find it, Lee's Pool Bar.

You'll see the pool first; it is fairly clean, tiled in blue and white and shaped like a banana. Then you'll see the bar; it is only a hut with a fake grass roof, but you'll know immediately that it does what it is supposed to do, serve alcohol. You might notice the fairy lights on the roof that we switch on in the evening. If it's your first holiday here, it could even remind you of a beachside bar on a luxury island, a further-away island, that you've seen in a film or something.

Or maybe you were expecting a pool table? Lee says we should get one. He thinks it would do fine in the sun but we can't afford one for now anyway. Like the chalkboard says, there is free Wi-Fi, when it works. We are far enough off the main road to block out the noise and the fumes wafting from the cars that crawl along to the beat of those summer hits that stick in your brain though you don't understand the words. The fat-trunked palm trees whisper a soothing breeze and the apartments surrounding the bar are bright white with green-painted shutters like all the buildings on the island. The black sand landscaping is manicured by the island men in blue boiler suits who whistle under their breath and watch you out of the corner of their eyes. So you'll sit down at a plastic table under a parasol and wait.

You will soon realise that the only problem with Lee's Pool Bar is Lee.

'Allo, darling,' he'll shout from his spot under the shade of the veranda.

Lee ruins it all, in his loud Hawaiian shirts that flap open to reveal his grey-haired pot belly, using his Jim Davidson chat-up lines on you in front of your kids or even your partner. You'll stiffen then, pull your kids to you or put a hand on your husband's knee, but he'll be looking around for a TV to watch the match on, so you'll stay out of politeness or exhaustion or the heat. You are on holiday so you will tolerate here what you would not tolerate at home.

'My old trouble and strife will pour ya a drink, get 'er off her fat arse. What'll ya 'ave?'

Then you'll look over at me, sitting there on my bar stool behind the counter, though I won't meet your eyes, because I'll know what's in them: pity. You think I haven't seen it a thousand times? I'll pour you a glass of San Miguel. I'll pass your kids over the cans of Coke, that you wouldn't allow them to drink at home, from the ice box under the counter. I won't make eye contact with them either. You'll drink quickly, squinting at the pool, as Lee wobbles beside you and stares at your chest.

If you decide to take your drink and stand up at the bar for a while to get away from him, I might tell you about my plan. I know you won't go to the police 'cause you'll think it's all part of an act or something. No one could be that stupid, you'll think, in this day and age. She could just leave, you'll think, there's divorce and there's cheap flights. But I'm not going anywhere, because truth be told I've nowhere to go. I came to Lee with nothing and he would make sure I went away with the same. And as you might have guessed by now, I want to stay, like you'll probably think you will too at some point during your holiday, maybe when your kids aren't whining or sunburnt or hungry or wired on Coca-Cola. It is a little piece of a paradise, to be fair, even here beside the pool. Lee is the serpent in the garden.

We met back home, in the bar where I worked, it wasn't a bit like this one of course. It was a proper English bar, dark and dusty with brass and leather horse tackle hanging on the walls that I had to polish every morning before I cleaned the toilets. I lived upstairs as part of the deal, in a room that didn't even lock properly. I had the use of the stainless steel kitchen and access to a shared sitting room where the owner's Alsatian sat panting. The owner, Barry (well he was the manager, truth be told), would always remark that it was an easy gig, running a bar, you could sit back and relax, he'd say, order other people around, hire and fire as you please. But I can't fire Lee, even though he does nothing except drink and frighten off the customers.

I'll change the name to Nora's Pool Bar, it's only right, it was all my idea to come here. It will be a safe haven for all, including me. Maybe I'll make it a women-only bar. A place women can come to, where they won't be bothered or even stared at. I'll have a strict policy about blokes, well, blokes who bother women. I might even have a bouncer. I'll lose a bit of weight, dye my hair, I'll wear a red flower behind my ear. I'll learn Spanish and buy one of those ruffled tops. Without him drinking all the profits I'll be able to afford a decent speaker system to play proper Spanish music; softly of course, so as not to disturb the neighbours. I'll serve up those big green olives and little baskets of bread, maybe even those little cold omelette tapas if I can find a genuine islander to tend the bar, not one of those Moroccans who turn up looking for work every other day.

I'll try to make it look like an accident, of course. I think a drowning would be best, a drunken drowning, but he's a strong bastard, Lee, especially when he's had a few. I might crush a few pills in his beer, it's easy enough to get them around here without a script, but not so many that they'd show up as suspicious on an autopsy or nothing. The police around here are well aggro, guns and truncheons always strapped to their belts, and the wife is probably the first one they'd suspect. Don't worry about me though, I plan to pin it on Dean.

I have tried to be a good stepmother to Dean, I really have, but he's had a spite on me since the first day I came home with Lee from the pub. He was around fifteen at the time and only stayed with Lee once a month at the most. So of course he was browned off that Lee had gone out and brought back a woman instead of spending a little quality time with his son. So it was easier to blame me, I suppose. I even saw him smirk one time Lee cracked me around the jaw for washing his white shirt pink.

Lee promised he would change, of course. After he'd flare up, he'd always say it wasn't his fault, he didn't know what came over him, that it was the car accident or the painkillers or the signing on that made him like he was. But it only got worse, even when he got the compo and then the all-clear in quick succession.

Now Dean sleeps on the pull-out sofa in the one-bedroom apartment that came with the lease. A growth spurt disguised the fat for a while, but his skin was always red and inflamed, he's never grown out of it. He was only supposed to come over for a week. He'd been living at his mum's up to then, him and his sister. I've never met Lee's daughter. He says his ex turned her against him, that she told a load of lies about him to get custody. Maybe I'll meet the daughter at the funeral, or invite her over after. Maybe I'll invite Lee's ex an' all.

The apartment is beside the bar so there is no escape from either of them, day or night. I really didn't think Dean would stay this long, there are no night-clubs here, no drugs except grass, no young people to speak of. Though Dean sometimes manages to pick up drunken girls on the strip. The ones who came here by accident mistaking it for one of the bigger islands or the ones who came with their parents for a free holiday. I hear them fumble in the dark.

I meet the girls in the morning sometimes, blondes more often than not, tattoos on their feet, black mascara streaked down their faces, hobbling out in their flip flops, blinded by hangovers. They look at me in disgust. They think their stomachs will never spread over their hips, that they will never let the roots show in their hair unless it's on purpose, that they will never wear tracksuits to work, that their belly piercings will save them from men like Lee.

I Give you my Hand

Katie McIvor

On the morning of the handfasting ceremony, two women came to the house and asked for my mother. I saw them approaching from the upstairs window. Their neat court shoes tamped down the moss of the garden path, and my stomach caved in with fear.

We heard the door; the clipped, bright voices of strangers; my mother's jangling laugh. I must have shuddered, because the hairdresser paused and put a hand on my shoulder, briefly, pressing into the vulnerable corner of clavicle. Then she resumed pinning my hair.

The house was giddy. My sister and the other bridesmaids darted up and down the stairs in monogrammed silk dressing gowns, their toes wriggling through the straps of their slippers, worm-like beneath pink fluff. I grew up in this house. My height markings decorate the kitchen doorframe, a rising stutter of blue pen chased and overtaken by the red of Serena's, for my sister outstripped me by two inches. Photographs of grandparents and the long dead line the stairs. There are lots of stairs: the house unfurls as though seeking the light, rooms stacked on rooms, ridged spines of staircases knotting the floors together. It's an old house. Its aching corners have borne witness to our tantrums, tears, shrieks and screams, whether in anger or in play. And, now, to this.

My mother came to fetch me. She said my name gently, as if awakening a baby, and then looked past me with an apologetic: 'If you're finished?'

The hairdresser nodded. Her smile in the mirror was wide and false. With my mother here, I understood, the touch to my shoulder had never happened. I smiled too and thanked her. She was pretty, prettier than me, and I found myself looking with envy at her hands as she clipped and folded her tools back into their black leather bag. For a mad instant I imagined crawling inside the bag with them, compressing my body to fit amongst the sprays and combs and claw-clips, refusing to come out.

There were over sixty pins in my hair. I felt them like tiny knives, a lace of daggers, holding my scalp in check.

My mother put her hand on my arm as we descended the stairs. On the landing was Serena, still in her dressing gown. With a little puff of air – 'Oh!' – she put a hand over her mouth and stepped back into the living-room doorway. In an armchair beyond, my father was taking comfort in a newspaper. I suddenly wanted to run to him, to say something, I don't know what. Instead I stared at Serena. Her face flushed. As I watched, the lacquer of her eyes brightened with nascent tears.

'Come, now, that's enough,' said my mother.

Her grip tightened. I became fixated at that moment on her other hand, the gloved hand, which drifted above the banister without quite touching it. I considered pitching myself forwards, toppling both of us, and wondered what that hand would then do: instinct over pain, or pain over instinct?

The two women were waiting in the parlour. An uncomfortable room for an uncomfortable process. I didn't want to go in. Something funny had happened to my breath and caused the flesh of my face to overheat. My mother patted my arm. I felt wild, blown up like a lost kite. I didn't want to embarrass her.

'It's just the fitting,' she whispered. 'It won't hurt.'

At that moment, I knew, Ven was sitting in the big house in the next village, his chin freshly scraped, his hair patted down with wax. He was probably eating a bacon sandwich and joshing with his brothers to ward off wedding-day nerves. Upstairs, his mother, the only woman of the house, would be painstakingly applying her makeup, the glove laid meat-like in her lap, listening to the laughter from below.

I want to be like her. I, too, want sons. I want to bask in my misfortune, proudly alone in my pain, sparing the next generation what befell me. Isn't that what motherhood means?

'Here's the blushing bride,' one of the women said.

I looked at them from inside a glass jar of fear. I was a child, shivering inside a snow globe. My mother propelled me towards the table.

'Sit, sit, sit,' said the other woman. 'Let's take a quick look.'

I had never seen women like them up close. They kept themselves apart. Their interests were loftier than ours. I wondered what it took, to choose life alone over marriage, over children, and wondered why I didn't have it. They wore ugly suits, cut to ridicule the waistline, in fabrics that were different but somehow alike: one green with golden flecks, one purple and grey. The soles of their shoes ground stickily on the wooden floor.

One of them swung a small briefcase onto the table. The other used both hands to pin me on a stool. My mother retreated to the doorway, wanting no part of this, or perhaps tactically blocking my exit. But I had no thoughts of bolting. My fear had relegated itself to a distant part of me, leaving only a blank sense of dislocation, a feeling of looking-down-upon, as though my body were no longer mine.

I watched with fascination as the women emptied the bag.

'Nothing to worry about,' one of them crooned. She laid out measuring tape, callipers, an adjustable harness of buckles and slim leather straps. 'Your new husband will find you irresistible, you know, in this.'

My memory jolted me into a day at the park, with Ven, back when we were courting. He had brought a picnic and tried to create a sense of romance, despite the sun that seared the skin of his neck and left him with a kerchief of red above the collar. We sat on the grass. Unseen tiny lifeforms itched into my skin. Nearby was a large group of girls, perhaps celebrating a birthday. They had baskets of food and plastic red cups that shone like blood in the sunlight.

One of the girls wore a glove. She sat in the midst of the group but seemed somehow held apart from it, her smile distant, as though her awareness lay in a different plane of reality. The glove floated just above her lap. I had heard that in the early days of handfasting, even the slightest touch brought pain. Girls would sleep with one wrist propped up against the headboard; you couldn't dangle your hand off the side of the bed, or the blood pooling into the constrictive glove caused it to swell unbearably.

I looked at Ven and saw he was watching the gloved girl. His lips were parted, his eyes vacant with unmistakeable lust. I felt cold and inadequate then, with my bare hand, my virginal fingers. I was incomplete, undesirable.

On the grass behind Ven an older man was lying down, perhaps asleep. I thought he might be a tramp. As I watched, I realised he was not sleeping. His eyes were narrowly open and he, like Ven, was gazing at the gloved girl. His hand moved busily beneath himself in a way that made me feel sick with embarrassment. I looked away, not towards Ven, not towards the gloved girl, but towards the shallow pond at the foot of the slope, where the heads of ducks moved like animatrons between the weeds.

The women held my arm in place as they fitted my glove. The leather was smooth, pale, beautiful. I felt a boiling rush of panic as they squeezed it onto my hand, but my mother had been right, it didn't hurt much, at least not yet. I breathed deeply and stared at the wall as the women fiddled with straps and buckles. The cuff around my wrist was uncomfortable, but that will be loosened with time, as the bones of my hand contract and shrink into their new shape. From now on, the burden of this hand's work will fall on others: sewing, typing, peeling vegetables, cutting fingernails. From now on, this hand will belong to my husband.

In an hour's time, I will walk down the aisle. There will be tiny knives in my hair and a gossamer veil over my face. Ven will fold back the veil and ceremoniously fit my glove. Our families will watch in respectful silence. They will see it as bad luck if Ven struggles with the buckles, good luck if my eyes water visibly. My sister will probably cry, and we will all ignore her racked, disbelieving sobs. After the ceremony, after Ven has taken my hand, there will be food and drink and dancing. When the night ends, Ven will take me home and remove over sixty pins from my hair. He will not remove the glove.

I'm told it gets less painful as you get older. With time, some people say, you can barely feel it at all.

Cleanliness is Next to Godliness

Laurence Lumsden

It was high time that someone said it. She put her teacup down abruptly and it clattered against the saucer.

'There's no need for you to wear that here,' she said.

The young woman looked up with a start, her soft features creased with alarm. The chatter around the table dissolved into silence.

'I'm sorry, Mrs. Gallagher. I don't understand?'

'Your veil. What is it that you call it? Your hijab! There's no need for it. Ireland is a free country. Women here are free to make their own choices, free to live their own lives.'

'Free to be cleaners,' cackled Eileen O'Rafferty. Mrs. Gallagher never took any notice of Eileen.

'Yes, Mrs. Gallagher,' said the young woman, her brown eyes magnified through thick glasses, her gaze clear and unblinking. 'So I choose to wear the hijab.'

'Oh, is it choosing that you're doing? Well now, it's not much of a choice if you've been brainwashed, is it?'

Eileen said something under her breath that Mrs. Gallagher didn't quite catch. She'd once overheard Eileen make a comment about her, something to the effect that her hair was dyed so black it made her face look startled, as if she was permanently caught in a photo flash. But she didn't really understand the remark as no one ever took her photo.

She picked up her cup and had a little sip of tea, pleased that the point about the veil had been made at last. On this January night in the Dublin offices of Taylor & Carson, specialists in family law, she'd granted the cleaning team a tea-break of fifteen minutes and not a second more. She'd recently been promoted to the role of team-leader at Kwick Kleen contract cleaners and she always gave precise instructions to her team-members. Pristine – she loved the antiseptic sound of that word. If someone didn't respond correctly they wouldn't last long, she could assure you of that. But she liked working with immigrants, they were so eager-to-please. She was quite satisfied with the young woman, Dirniz or Dornaz or something like that, who'd joined the team before Christmas. Pakistani probably. Mrs. Gallagher had come across many of them when she'd lived in London all those years ago.

All those years. A lump came into her throat and she put the teacup down, gently this time, though she couldn't prevent her hand from trembling. Her life in London was the very thing she did not want to remember, not tonight, and she swallowed hard to make the memory go away again. When her mother had taken to her deathbed she'd had to come home to Dublin to look after the old woman, and that was all there was to it. She'd heard nothing from London since, not a single reply to her cards or letters, until this morning. God's ways were mysterious.

The overhead lights of the kitchen buzzed like trapped flies and she allowed herself a soundless sigh. But what in the name of God was Eileen O'Rafferty blabbering on about now?

'Durnaz, have you made any New Year's resolutions?'

'Well, I intend to finish my studies in March and then I hope to be able to find a better job.'

'Studies,' said Mrs. Gallagher. What studies are these now?'

'I am going to be a programmer,' said Durnaz with a shy smile. 'I appreciate this job, Mrs. Gallagher, but I want to get a better one to support my family so that we can move to a nicer flat.'

'Ah go on, Durnaz, tell us about your family,' said Eileen, ignoring the withering look from her team-leader.

'Well, my husband works in a Halal butcher's shop on Clanbrassil Street. Our lovely little boy, Hamza, is three years old. He's already started to read English, and is learning to …'

'It's time to get back to work,' interrupted Mrs. Gallagher. 'Eileen, please stack the dishwasher and make sure this kitchen is pristine for Mr. Taylor and his associates.'

'Don't you worry now, Mrs. G,' said Eileen, 'the kitchen will be spotless. And Durnaz and me will have the toilets gleaming and smelling of roses for their delicate pink bottoms.'

Durnaz put a hand over her mouth to stifle a giggle.

Mrs. Gallagher turned away and walked quickly into Mr. Taylor's corner office, closing the heavy door behind her. She always cleaned this office alone – no one else did it properly. She turned on the vacuum cleaner, then took the letter from the pocket of her grey smock. The white envelope had startled her that morning, stark on the well-scrubbed floorboards of her hall, next to a flyer from another new kebab shop. She'd waited so long for a reply from London but when she saw the Royal Mail postmark and the stamp with the image of the Queen she'd known right away that something was wrong. Her hands shook again now as she re-read it for the umpteenth time, still wondering if there was something she'd missed.

London, December 30th

Dear Rose,

We haven't been in touch for such a long time, but my darling Timothy always appreciated the cards you sent every Christmas. You were his favourite Irish nanny. Timothy passed away last April. He fought cancer for several years with great courage and was quite peaceful in the end. I thought you'd like to know that he never forgot you.

Yours sincerely,
Helen Saunders

Mrs. Gallagher had thought of posting a Mass card, but then she remembered that Mrs. Saunders had no patience for what she called 'Catholic superstitions'. Besides, it was too late – Timothy had been dead for months. She swallowed hard, but her sobs bubbled up like suds. 'My lovely little boy,' she said to no one. The vacuum cleaner droned on, and her team heard nothing.

On a breezy night in March the cleaning team was giddy ahead of the St. Patrick's Day holiday, and spirits were high at the tea break when there was no sign of their team-leader. After twenty minutes Durnaz got up and peered around the door of Mr. Taylor's office. Mrs. Gallagher was lying on the thick carpet.

Durnaz shouted, 'Eileen, please call an ambulance.'

Mrs. Gallagher tried to sit up, but the young woman put a gentle yet firm hand on her shoulder.

'Please lie still, Mrs. Gallagher, help will be here soon.'

They were greeted at St. James's hospital by a throng of fussing medical staff. But once it became clear that she hadn't suffered a stroke, Mrs. Gallagher was left to wait on a trolley in a noisy corridor with all sorts of people coming and going. She wouldn't have felt safe there alone, but Durnaz sat on a chair beside her like a guardian angel, solemn and silent.

Finally a nurse announced that a ward bed had become available.

'Go home now, Durnaz,' she said. 'I'll be grand.'

'Mrs. Gallagher, are you sure? No one should be alone when they are ill.'

'Go on home. Your little boy needs you.'

She was surprised at how lonely she was when Durnaz had left. There were blood tests and examinations, but mostly she just lay on the bed and waited. Time yawned, fatigue weighed on her, and the hours stretched into a drawn-out day. She knew that the doctors would do their best but she was under no illusions about what they'd find. The pain in her back, the inability to eat, she was ready for the diagnosis of cancer. If it was God's plan then so be it. Her funeral arrangements were already made and her will was written. Her nephew would inherit the old house, although God knows he didn't need it. She prayed it wouldn't end up as one of those Airbnb places.

An unexpected thought came to her: Durnaz would appreciate the house. It would change her life. The house would become a family home, with a garden for her son to play in. The more she thought about it the more it seemed the right thing to do. Mr. Taylor could easily change the will. She imagined walking into the office she knew so well, saying, 'Yes, Mr. Taylor, I'm leaving my house to Durnaz Khan. It's a Pakistani name, D-U-R-N-A-Z.'

She slept well that second night in the hospital, better than on any night in the months since the letter had arrived. In the morning her nephew came to visit, wearing a suitably grave expression.

'Is there anything I can do for you, Aunty Rose?'

She was all set to ask him to drive her to the offices of Taylor & Carson, but now she hesitated. She couldn't involve him in arranging his own removal from her will.

'No, nothing, thank you. I'm grand.' She'd have to find another way, maybe through a social worker in the hospital. But she was determined that she wouldn't die until her will had been changed and Durnaz's future secured.

After her nephew left, a doctor arrived at her bedside, his face dark and serious.

'We've reviewed the results of your tests, Mrs. Gallagher.' He spoke with a melodic Indian accent, pronouncing the soft *gh* of her name like a *j*, rolling the *r* exotically. Mrs. Gallajerrr. 'I can reassure you that there is no sign at all of any cancer.'

'I'm sorry, doctor, but I don't understand.'

'Yes, you are cancer free, but you are rundown and underweight. You haven't been looking after yourself.'

'I see.'

'We shall have to fatten you up with our wonderful hospital food,' he continued, breaking into a broad smile.

She thought she might die of embarrassment.

On a mild night just after Easter, the cleaners were on their break.

'Wouldn't you miss Durnaz all the same,' said Eileen O'Rafferty, and there was a chorus of 'ahh yeahs' from around the table.

Mrs. Gallagher blew on her teacup.

'You weren't here for her last day, Mrs G,' continued Eileen. 'I was talking to her over the weekend. She loves her new job. She's not the only one wearing a hijab either, but I'd bet that none of the others have ever had to make a living from cleaning toilets.'

'No, I suppose not.'

'She was a bit taken aback to be working with a trans woman. But as I said to her, on the inside we've all got more in common than we realise.'

Mrs. Gallagher took a sip of tea.

'Anyway, she did a great job in Mr. Taylor's office while you were off. Pristine, as you'd say yourself.'

'Well I'll be cleaning it tonight.'

She walked into the corner office and began vacuuming, surprised at how proud she felt of the young woman. It would have been nice to stay in touch, to see her little boy grow up, but it didn't seem possible. She wouldn't be able to send Christmas cards to a Muslim home.

She switched off the vacuum cleaner. Some differences were just too big to overcome, she said to herself. But the silence in the office pressed on her with the weight of all the dreary years and the feeling of pride curdled inside her. There was nothing and no one left for her now, and it was far too late for anything to be done about it.

The door behind her opened.

'Are you alright, Mrs. G? It got very quiet for a minute there.'

'Just finish the toilets please, Eileen.'

Eileen left again and Mrs. Gallagher allowed herself a sigh. It was only a moment of weakness in the hospital, that's all. It hadn't meant anything and there was no harm done in the end, but she had a bitter taste in her mouth. She pulled fiercely on the hose of the vacuum cleaner and dragged it from the office. Then she reached back, switched off the lights, and closed and locked the heavy door.

Stars

Peter Adair

The beautiful people all are dying,
the names and faces we called our own.
How they fall away without trying.

On the airways you hear them sighing,
they leave the stage for parts unknown.
The beautiful people all are dying,

their reedy voices still denying
hands that lose the microphone.
How they fall away without trying.

The sad toll leaves us crying:
immortals, though only on loan.
The beautiful people all are dying.

For moments, stunned in the rush of buying,
we hear their last accusing moan.
How they fall away without trying.

Our gods are dead, there's no denying.
We bow our heads, silent, alone.
The beautiful people all are dying.
How they fall away without trying.

A Note on Place Names

Liam Aungier

Do Bhrian Ó Daimhín, file

English is our *lingua franca* – our fluency
The small change of a parlance we expend
At village shop and public house, a currency

Always on our tongue, its toothed edge
Worn smooth with common use,
Rounded by our frequency of exchange.

The land remembers an older language:
A vernacular that came with Iron Age tools,
With cursive art, new gods, the Celtic Age.

Only fold out the concertina of a map
Or take notice of gesturing road signs
To read the poetry of a landscape:

Church of the Oak, the Dancing Stone,
The Salmon's Leap. *Cill Dara,*
Cloch an Rince, Léim an Bhradáin.

The Drunken Gardener

Ivy Bannister

Moon lours.
His blood is a flow of vodka and orange.
He climbs the black alder that thrusts
towards the sky, hacks at a branch that cracks,
then drops with a thundering crash. See
him tumble after, grab at the earth, compress
its granules in dark lonely hands, assault
the roses – Cherry Parfait, Catherine McAuley –
their soft velvet's in bits. Listen
to the laughter that boils from his lips.
How he wants, feel his want, he's consumed
with desires – a thyrsus to grip, a leopard to straddle.
His mouth fills with grapes, vines trail from his ears,
with a howl he whips his wisteria tail.

A cigarette smoulders, hot and bright.
My soul, he mutters, *isn't made for the light.*

Inseparable

Gerard Beirne

Like rivers meeting, or fear in the presence of thoughts,
melancholia dispersed through the confluence of all that was us.

No matter. The survivors gather what they can
while those who ran cast leaves across a treeless land.

What we held towards the light was dulled by inclement weather.
I am happy to have known what we never knew together.

The wonder in our lives on which we could not agree.
The abulia of our conscience lacking no morality.

There was worship, and there was praise for the day of wrath.
We were inseparable. Cut from the same cloth.

Silent Reading Time

Peter Branson

Catholic Primary, aged 8

Her 'Silence!' mime, right index finger press
from nose to lips, picture a clock on high,
the minute hand delayed at six, our lunch-
break Angelus, watched kettlefuls, betrayed,
time stalled. Some hunker down to read. The rest,
resigned, mask-like, our inner faces one
slow stifled scream, eyes chaste as sunbeams in
a cloudy sky, day dream, the page unturned.
Our teacher feigns due vigilance, her mind
elsewhere, a dinner date, which dress to wear.
Mum overheard her gossiping at Mass.
So if he asks her back, coffee or wine,
good Catholic girl, her matching underwear
a red for danger sign, will she decline?

Seers & Mortals

Laura Treacy Bentley

Lincoln predicted his death in April.
He dreamed he heard muffled sobbing
and wandered from room to room

until he discovered a shroud-covered body
in an East Room bed guarded by soldiers.
'The President is dead,' a soldier told him.

If Booth's derringer had jammed,
Lincoln might have lived to dream another day.

To prove his strength,
Houdini let a student punch him in the stomach.
He died on Halloween of a ruptured appendix,

unable to escape the shackles of death.
If Houdini hadn't bragged
he could take on such blows,

he might have lived
to escape again.

Twain was born when Halley's Comet
strobed across the sky.
'I came in with Halley's Comet,'

and proudly predicted he would
go out with it in April 1910.
If he hadn't been so sure of his fate,

he might have cheated death
to write another story.

If my grandmother who practised
numerology and palm reading,
had married Herman, her first love,

I wouldn't be here,
typing this poem
under April's troubled sky

to dream
another day.

Permission

Lauren Camp

On our way to a park in this brazen city,
we are walking along the asphalt toward a gate,
a place to slip inside, through
corners. We've done lots of other walking and one night
of dancing and boozing; those hours
a whisk of energy: the herbalist,
the administrator, the woman who could bend and me.
Done leaping we Uber-ed back to sleep.
Now a day later with the bendable woman
in this crackling city, moist
and unlustred, but with arching
roses clustered in gray places, the first start
of a solace to the east
and north, past histories and thresholds
where wind sleeks lightly with a porch painted white.
Trees stand and in them by turns birds. We hear
each tiny satisfied heart. Into the gate
and within the park, a soft blue ball parries
its pleasure and pine needles. A satellite
of bees chorus in purple petals, a fragrance left
from their ripples. It's fine to be snug
in a landscape where people's hips curve beneath
tuning kinglets, where locust trees shuffle their tufty branches.

How we have nearly forgotten the normal.
A man holds his baby daughter. I am undone
by her red hairbow.
The sky parses steeples in silver.
A clock tower finds its beseeching order.
Today needs only a chance to lean in
to each bush's rapture and boredom. Nothing much
is breathtaking. The homeless remain
numerous. A bell keeps ringing
a spectacular scent of spring. Its musty sigh.

Peacock in the Car Park

Louise G Cole

A day so dismal, no puddles glint in the headlight sweep
picking out a line of shopping trolleys awaiting a coin,
and the push across rain-soaked supermarket tarmac.

I slam the car door, wince at the cold slosh against my skin,
sense I am being watched, turn to see a peacock, sheltering
as best he can, huddled in the lee of a long wooden fence.

He's feet away from me. But really, a peacock in the car park?
I fear the day I've had, the week, the month, the year
has tricked me into hallucination. I blink fast, he stares back.

I look around but there is no-one else nearby. No-one
viewing an exotic bird, only me, holding my breath
as with a shake, quills quivering, he unfurls the fabulous.

How does he know I need this moment, this feather-flare
to persuade me to carry on, to carry on, to carry on,
to forget about so many things that don't really matter?

Because here, only a posing peacock's iridescence matters,
plumage of blue, turquoise, eyes of purple staring me down.
He turns to catch the light that isn't there, and then back

but his gaze doesn't leave mine, he's courting adulation.
I mutter soft incantations of appreciation, feel the need
to explain: I have an important thing to do – shopping.

But I will return with treats, something worthy of a god,
for surely, he's hungry? Isn't everyone? That's why I'm here,
to harvest a week's worth of food from shop shelves,

I have a family to feed. When eventually I assail the aisles,
I think I should have taken pictures, phone-proof of a reality
casually confirmed by the checkout girl: he's a regular,

lives nearby, accepts gifted breadcrumbs, popcorn, pastry.
Outside, rain and darkness fall, but I tread lightly to my car,
scanning for signs of life, disappointed to see he's vanished.

Loading leaden shopping bags, everything is dark and wet
until a flash at my feet, and I peel a single soaked feather
from among the fag ends and crisp packets, fallen leaves.

I hold the feather close, remember and forget, begin to weep.

How to be Bog

Rachael Davey

Be discreet in all you do. Grow quietly.
Remember rain is everything. Rain and your dead.
Hold them lightly. Hold them. Your dead become you.

Be modest always. Choose colour with care.
Wear muted autumn shades but allow some adornment.
In Spring, favour brimstone butterflies,

acid hues in small swarms.
Damselfly, cottongrass and cranberry draw little attention.
Dragonflies only in moderation.

Remember water. And your dead. Keep them near
and you will flourish. Cover yourself with shawls of sphagnum.
Add lichen, myrtle, the lightest spangle of heather.

Let your pools lie dark and still, but stud their edges
with garnets of sundew. Eels may caress your watery places,
otters lie close. Make space for the brown hare

to nestle your breast. Hold your living close, your dead closer.
Remember, rain is everything. Rain, and your dead.
Breathe quietly. Grow slowly. Hope men overlook you.

Tolka Cottages

Maurice Devitt

I'd dander on the doorstep, while she went
to get money for the pools, crane my neck
to see inside the hall, a muzzle of darkness.
The waft of fried bread and turf ushered her
from the scullery at the back, my eyes drawn
to the torn piping on the pocket of her
sleeveless housecoat. She passed me the change,
door closed quickly in my face. Sometimes
in summer we'd see her lying on the apron
of lawn out front, clipping the grass with a
scissors and talking to herself. When we played
football on the road outside, she threatened to cut
the ball in four halves and though we marvelled
at the maths, it felt like a spell that shouldn't be ignored.

A Jigsaw for James Merrill

Maitreyabandhu Dharmachari

from 'The Covid Coda'

Lunch.   'I can't get myself going today'
my mother tells me, breathless on the phone,
'I couldn't face the shops.' She's round the corner
with her wheelie-walker breaking up

the tedium of days all locked together
(hard to tell apart like the puzzle's
vacant skies), inspecting what the council's
done with the flowerbeds and freshly painted

Henley-in-Arden sign that takes her back
to marriage, tittle-tattle and pork pies.
The puzzle waits: Anne Hathaway's Cottage Garden –

tea rose, celandine … She's gathered all
the straw into a single grey-backed pile,
against her loneliness, for thatching time.

Some Definitions

Daragh Fleming

'he's embarrassing himself,' is what you said to him about me. when you sent it, you didn't think I'd find out, but he couldn't help himself. he sent it to me and I sent it back to you. one round of Chinese Whispers and here we are. and by 'we' I mean me and you, and by 'you' I mean you and him, sitting in the apartment that we picked out, talking about how embarrassing I am, forgetting that he used to be me.

The History of a Glove

Deborah H. Doolittle

Whose hand it once embraced
is missing both
its loveliness and its grace.

Gravity took it, or was it
the wind?
Others flutter softly around it

without a glance: hobnail boot,
stiletto heel, high top sneaker.
Its chances of being found out

as part of a match
are grim. Still it retains the slim
shape of its former self;

like a limp balloon, a deflated inner
tube, which have nothing on it.
Its partner lies

in wait somewhere in the bottom
of a drawer, tucked within
a deep pocket of a bulky coat

in the back of some closet,
or swept under the rug;
that's where it weeps for her

and no one else. Silently, utterly
alone, overwhelmed by the immensity
of time and distance.

Rodent

Maryellen Hodgins

For Grainne

In the morning quietness
of the garden, a rat appeared
slipping under the garden
gate

I watched it, the small
humped creature appearing
and disappearing in the wet
grass

Till it stopped suddenly, I
crossed the garden to where
it was, found it, lying flat
out

Its nose twitched, sensing
someone was near, still
it did not move, I knew it
was dying

Most likely in pain, it had
come to my garden to die
I placed a dish of water close
to his whiskers

It lifted its head, looked at me
for an instant, then dropped its
snout to the water, taking a
few sips

I waited, watching the small
movement of its breathing
I could have stroked its wet
coat, but thought it better
not to

I think it knew it was not
alone, this least favoured
of all God's creatures.

Raven's Lullaby

Nicola Geddes

We hear whispers
in jade and violet and silver
we, who are unafraid of the dark

Long before the black feathers formed themselves
on your naked skin, before you broke out
of the mottled shell and into your blind staggering days
before that clutch was even laid
in the wool-felted twig cup
we heard in your sheen
cobalt, amethyst and deep sea green

Our wings span across the worlds
circle the ocean
circle the cloud
circle around the ground

Spring is in the bare hawthorn and black-budded ash
here are the murmurings of the not yet
Ours is a way of seeing in the blackest of feathers
the true colours of magic.

Heart of the Fox

Rebecca Gethin

My father told me the story of the Spartan boy
and the fox more than once – about the boy who stole a cub

and bundled it inside his tunic. He said nothing
to the centurion who addressed him as the creature

chewed and gnawed through his flesh to his heart
with its shearing teeth. The boy dropped dead

and the creature escaped. My father admired
the Spartan spirit and I thought he expected this of me.

Now I think it was he who had a secret, holding it
inside his shirt for years while it clawed at his vitals

and he kept quiet. What this was I'll never know.
His heart went the way of that boy. An old man

I met in the Alps whose knobbly hand dove-tailed into mine
said he'd known my family well. When I asked him

about my father who was in the Resistance up there
he said, *He was too dangerous to know.*

Grass

Mark Granier

Bray Head, 2020

I don't think I've ever seen grass

this luxuriant, a seedy, waist-high crop
cresting over, deepening the thin trodden paths,
(two children bright as crayons, walking a dog
through the frothy, sibilant sea).
                       Rampant wild grass –
with a light breeze searching for a parting –
that keeps the whole slope weaving and unweaving.

Bend closer, and each shivering tip rises,
tapestry-bright, distinct as a headdress
or a working quill, as if the field were breathlessly
inscribing its own epic.
                What are you –

Tufted Hair? Canary? Lyme? Meadow Fescue?
Crested Dog's-Tail? Meadow Cat's-Tail? Common Bent?

I must now add to my ignorance of birdcalls
this illegible grass, flattened here and there with forms
where families had picnicked or lovers rolled –

Bespoke grass, tailor-made for a doze,
grass to lose a million needles in
or find them. Grass working its shuttle loom.
Grass to make wishes on. Grass with no design
other than to be grass

feathering its own nest. Grass like us.

Clonmoylan Summer

Margaret Hickey

Vetch and apple-scented eglantine,
Wild honeysuckle and Queen Anne's lace,
Spike and umbellifer jut up from the tangle,
Stitching themselves into every summer hedgerow.

Brambles, sprigged with innocent mauve flowers,
Thrust out barbed arms to rip the passer-by.
Showy convolvulus, angelic in white,
Grows from a thread and strangles all it finds.

Daisies stud the ground with milky buttons,
The purple clover straddles the white:
Grasses and dandelions grown four foot high,
Dip and jumble and wave in the meadows.

Overhead, the Doppler effect of a honeybee,
And a high metallic chipping, as unnamed birds
Squabble up high. Beech trees cut jigsaw shapes
Into a hazy, blue-grey sky; the sun diffuses.

A plank bridge, weathered to an ashy grey,
Spans the narrow cut, its water so still
Green chenille algae skin its surface.
A dragonfly drops silent on a lilypad.

The scent of meadowsweet hangs in the verges
And every green in nature shows its face:
The glossy green of holly, the mossy green of dock,
With the nettle sharpest, most precise of all.

Birch trees slant and thwart, their bark forever peeling.
Ivy dresses, softens drystone walls.
A pumpkin-coloured fungus, wide as a dinner plate,
Grows in steps at the base of a fallen oak.

Scurrying through mazes of undergrowth,
Centipedes, inexplicably pressed for time,
While spiders, dissatisfied with yesterday's work,
Weave new and better webs afresh.

A Photo my Blink Took

Bob Hicok

Nothing lasts,
the waves say
on the way out,
having asked,
Will you love me
when they arrived,
and between, for less
than a second,
nothing moves,
not my heart
or the sky
or the dog
who wants to
bite the waves
and hold on
to them a little
less than I do.

Clear

Fred Johnston

This first hour of the morning the light is pure
That's to say, the chug and smoke and weather haven't stained it
From leaf to open book lying on a chair
The light is almost silver, everything is so utterly *there*
No dust falls through it
The only time of the day all things are sure –

The postman's rattle through the gate
Is the first assault. The dogs yap like gunshots, a first rain falls
A first rain turning to flat lead the glister on the windowglass
A varnished leaf takes a droplet's weight and its trespass
Shivers like a touched nerve and hauls
Itself off on a wet arc of wind. The postman's late.

Poems in Search of a Home

Breda Joyce

Sprawled on the steps outside *An Chomhairle Filíochta*
poems huddle together to find a way
to come to terms with their exclusion.
They hail passers-by, promise to hide away
until further polished up and clean,
start rehab to recover
from this addiction to be seen

On hard ground they rearrange themselves
into new formations: swop stanzas,
delete adjectives, forego adverbs,
in a precarious world make all articles indefinite,
go on a diet of plain verbs and nouns.
And as for conjunctions, use dashes instead –
they have no business hanging around.

Time to strip off more layers. No point
in denying editorial advice –
their torment appeased in another's eyes.
They must believe in themselves, stay focused
on what exactly they mean to say,
hold out for the possibility
of publication some other way.

Tonight, they'll be back here again,
close up zippers, shut their eyes
against a world that makes them homeless.
Tomorrow they will seek new shelter,
(they won't make a fuss),
hope to slip between covers
try harder to adjust.

Fire Alarm

Claire-Lise Kieffer

After Ilya Kaminsky

       I smelled the smoke.
It waited for us on the first floor, as thick
as a bad dream. It had eaten plastic
and a fake leather couch. It had the inside
of a living room on its breath. Outside,
alarms ablaze, the neighbours turned out
like contents of a handbag were glazed
in blue and red lights. We had left the cats,
thinking it was just a drill. We grew afraid
for their small lives.
              (beat.)
I hadn't read
about the war, not yet. But back upstairs,
when we had cried, and plied the cats with treats,
I scrolled through bad news. In early dreams,
they commingled with our minor scare.
Yes, we are the ones living happily
during the war. Possibly, you are thinking
that this age is the most privileged yet,
but our future is burning and last night,
I smelled the smoke.

Official Business

Brian Kirk

These are the duties you must undertake
with a clear conscience and a civil smile,
armed with a laptop and a limp handshake,
the histories of tenants housed in files.
The homeless and the helpless plead their case
in writing or by telephone; meanwhile
you see nothing but the commonplace,
a story told so many times before.
Your fingers on the keys depress backspace
until the form is wiped and through a trapdoor
the client disappears, becomes a void,
a problem solved, an applicant no more.
Work such as this can never be enjoyed,
but you are blessed, being gainfully employed.

Graveyard: Morning

Robert Leach

It's dawning
In this walled-in world,
Where green, flop-headed grasses sway
And tight, upright slabs stand,
Rigid, erect.

A pliable slug
Drags its black, slimy way
Over still-dark earth,
A blackbird jabs and stabs
At perhaps a fleeing worm,
Small birds
Whistle, pipe, chirp.

And one, dull brown warbler,
Lyrical, melodious,
Alights on a grim unmoving grave,
Sings, now, for ever.

Seasoning

Noelle Lynskey

August, a month of slowness,
lazy wasps hang about, blackberries brushing green to red.
It catches you – the sideways sun peppering the lush thickets – then the rush
back-to-school before the month has turned herself over to the 1st.
No break to pick the ripe berries, to lick their purple
gleam before the jar is sealed.
No time to stay up late, bathe in the silver night, the harvest moon.
The last chance of a dip
in the chilly salt of sea
and vinegared chips, missed.
What hurry is on them? Let them off
for a few days more,
see them grow another inch.

On a Christmas Morning

V.P. Loggins

I could hear them slapping wings
against the surface of black water
before I saw them there, paddling

in unison as the light was spreading.
Canada geese floating by the dozen.
I counted and found their number

to be thirty-three and thought of Christ,
this being a Christmas morning,
the number seeming significant, though

doubtless arbitrary, something I sensed
I was choosing to believe in. Then
I heard what seemed the faint tinkling

of a fountain when I saw the outsider,
a cormorant serenely observing, low
in the water, so similar, so diffcrent

than the others, like Satan, I thought,
shape-shifted in Milton's Eden.
Suddenly the cormorant dove

and the desperate shad began to emerge
by the hundreds, cracking
the glassy surface of this watery paradise.

When the black bird rose from the depth,
its hooked beak clinched a fish like
a silver secret flashing in the gray light.

And as the water began to settle
it seemed to catch the sky above it
and hold it there like a piece of heaven.

Wet Monday in Galway

James Martyn Joyce

The sad and the bad claim the sleep-washed town,
the sheen of black rain the length of Quay Street,
mangled bin bags spew onto wet pavements,
grounded seagulls cowering in doorways.
Outside coffee shops and pubs, in ones and twos
men lean into it.

Conversation is limited to nods and blinks,
By Murphy's Bar, older men stare off into yesterday
while the younger ones, frantic with need,
sidle close to whisper possibilities.
Rain, at a slant, gathers in coffee cups
brown-stained, empty.

At Saint Nicks, in the medieval graveyard,
a young man, bewildered, follows a bird,
mimicking flight for anyone who cares.
On Shop Street, three American ladies,
sharing steel-wool hairstyles, usher each other
towards The Hardiman Hotel.

At the pedestrian lights, they pause,
the horn-rimmed dowager in the lead
turning to address the others: 'See,
It's not that hard to get a MAN.'
She shouts; then, she spells it out,
'Yes, a M-A-N!'

She enters the traffic, still on red, turns midstream,
'a M-A-N', she stresses again, arms raised,
magician style: like it might be possible to conjure up
such a being, on a wet Monday, in Galway, in April,
downpour weather, despair writ large on bleak streets,
Each-Desperate-Letter-Underlined.

Arguing Into Resistance

Karen J McDonnell

'... argue into those resistances.' – Eavan Boland

Depleted, unsure in the dark.
All that white space to fill
and internal arguments unquenched.

Comes the instruction:

Fish the outrageous fire.
Throw out lines
into the new day.

What surfaces, what is landed,
is a grace-gift;
the dawn's benevolence.

After the churning of nightmares
and fevered reveries,
word-shoals will beach

– tumbling upon themselves
like stones grumbling
at the tidal zone.

Root

Kate McHugh

On a walk in Barna Woods I see a tree split in two
near the mouth, the broken part lolling like a tongue stretched
out into a bin emptied for vomit on New Year's Day,
after a taxi home with a driver who asks me where I'm from
originally because he doesn't find me Galwegian.
Living in France, are ya? I can hear it in your accent alright,
not from around here anyway.

My mother tells me the tree has been like that a few months
while we stand observing how a third of it bends low towards the earth
like the slant of a 6 an old maths teacher used to scrawl
before I run into her in town where she talks of the twinge in my accent.
France now, is it? Sure, if I didn't know ya I would
never have guessed Galway.

Feet pull us forward and the tree is left waiting open to the wind,
oak insides bare like my back under the movement of a masseuse whose
fingers feel out a pattern on my skin, searching for seeds and their shoots,
and when she finds me unearthed and separate in the wood
asks what brings me to Galway and I tell her this is home.
    Really?

Funny Girl

Alan McMonagle

She cracks me up, this five-year-old
of the chocolate eyes and matching teeth
as she ballerinas to the mirror
to recite her catalogue of grievances.

The waxy bell living inside her ear.
A satsuma that burns her throat.
My halo is broken, she fervently declares,
and the letter F apart, Fridays

are a catastrophe. It's not funny, she says,
giving me her assassin pout.
And I tell her the story
about the man in edible stilettos

searching theatrically for the mini-skirt
he must wear to the ball or else
his life is over. What about my life?
she says, shrugging haughty

and hands-on-hips laments
how everything has changed
since the roaring boy turned up
receiving now this, now that,

and all she has is the letter F.
And I'm off again, coughing my laughter
all over her mismatched shoes and inky dress.
It's not funny, she says, her glaring face

piling on the trouble coming my way
and I switch on the music
and she is instantly giddy
when she hears her song

pulls me from the lazy chair,
has us waltzing a rumba
as she begins to tell me
all about her love affair
with the letter F.

Brine

Nicole Morris

Face first and somehow wet with salt, the air had mass to it,
I stood at the southernmost start of the sea in the bottom boot

Of Ireland, January with fog that lay in sheets first at eye level, then
Bent to the ground, a bow or curtsey or buckling of will

It wasn't fog, I knew that, these were clouds running down
North to the South, in mourning veils and drizzled to meet the sea

At County Kerry, my own mouth open in a quiet keening
Audible only to ears tuned to the grief note, still though

I was in love with the saline of it, salient as blood on the
Salted slip of my lip, rain as respiration, respirate me

More than mist, fatter than the sky, this ocean of tears
And the sun, hiding behind her mother's skirt, shy-casting shade

I came here to grieve, and I wasn't let down by the damp,
It held me with both arms, whispering hush now

And I didn't mind the way my bones were made cold
Beneath muscle, how the wool did nothing to warm my feet

A magpie in flight with her blue-black line of praise
A heifer in her curly winter coat and my fingers exposed

At the tips of my sleeves and the sand so still against the tide
You could almost forget that a child drowned here,

Well, not *here* here, but near enough, round the bend and back
Upwards, going East, then North again, on Burrow Beach

In July, a boy, a pull, a catch in the current, and then no more
Tippy-toed out to deep waters, joining the ghosts of ghosts floating

Irish Sea, Atlantic-bound and then no more, not here, he was a stranger to me,
But I knew that baby, I knew that child in the way that all mothers are mothers

To all, especially in death, and it's his mama's weeping making waves
Now, high tide now, a brine for the broken now

For Bradley Lulendo, forever aged 13, who drowned at Burrow Beach in Sutton, north County Dublin, July 2022 while playing with friends. He could not swim, so he tried to stay at a depth where his toes stayed on the sea floor.

A Hard Night's Work

John Reinhart

Walking Clancy, we step over
Mrs. Hitchens
curled up, sleeping soundly
on the sidewalk,
tired, I assume, from her late night —
full moon and all —
pass Mr. Wiley hurrying home
just before sunrise,
shivering under his hooded
woollen cloak.

The newspaper delivery is happening
like clockwork —
Sally's gears must be well-oiled
today. 'Good morning!' I greet
the neighbour at the end
of the road. I've never caught his name —
sounds Hungarian — and, between you and me,
he always seems a little bleary-eyed,
a little undead, if you'll excuse the expression,
but neighbours are neighbours and people are
just people

people going about life,
just like me and Clancy,
who stops to sniff ... something,
probably nothing, though he's
adamant that there's something there.
If only I could see the world
through a dog's nose,
to know why he's got to stop
at every tree, every post,
as if those things too warranted
greeting

but what do I know,
just that we both need a stretch
after our night keeping
the demons
at bay

Word Cave

Lorna Shaughnessy

After Paul Celan

Grief empties words of all their intimacies.
They will be hollow now, like this house without its contents,
missing the sounds and textures of your dressing-table:
the ridged edges of a comb, click of compact mirror,
stickiness of a forgotten mint.
Like dust motes when we pull out the furniture, they hover,
uncertain where to land, whether to land at all.
The drawer without its jumbled contents is so forlorn
it echoes with the ghosts of candle stub ub ub,
broken watch strap ap ap and tube of glue ue.
I have mined this motherlode so long I cannot tell
which words are yours and which are mine. And yet,
when I open my mouth in these empty rooms today
only breath sounds, breath with no accent, no provenance,
all the words we shared evicted.
I need to find a word cave, somewhere to hibernate a while
and line its walls with the salvaged sounds of home,
tether all the last words, keep them close
then dream them over and over, listening
for the tones beneath the tones.

The City

Jo Slade

I have cast a spell on the city I have fixed this time and place
the way it is this moment a kind of death to hold time back
I stand on a bridge and watch the river flow into the loved line
and beyond to a quiet side — quietness between here now
and this steel grey sky brightening slowly snow
soft stillness of white a dull white falling and I want to find
in this mix of pallid water and sky in the wide arc darkening
inside me a name for this quietness —
and to name something that is here or not here water
like a secret pawing me if I could enter if I could wade under
the heart eyed and crystal like silt hardening in the bitter cold
a pale fog hugs the surface and way out a blaring up light
first vague hint of umber drifts the sky smooths the edges
the slow eye moves under the day exhales an icy breath
and etches time to winter's glass

Bring Me Your Hurt

Breda Spaight

after Ellen Bass

Bring me your hurt, my love,
unfold it like the wings of a caged bird – the sun parakeet,
the peacock, shimmering sapphire and emerald
of hummingbirds. Show me
the oiled hooves of the unicorn,
how you section the mane between wither and forelock
to braid rosebud plaits. Allow me to follow your finger
with my finger as you chart the spiral of its horn.
Shrug it from your shoulders like a shawl, my love,
the cashmere fragrant with your body's perfume.
Let butterflies flutter from your mouth.
In the dense wood of your pain, I will hew the rampant holly,
hack the curling stems of bramble and make a path. There
I will walk with you until branch and briar
arch to our shape.

How to Let a Wild Thing Go

Bobbie Sparrow

Did you trap it? If so, reflect.
Get on your knees and stain
the taupe silk dress you bought
in error after two glasses of wine.
Let the dark earth mark you,
don't cry, you are not a cloud.
Did you offer shelter? If so, reflect.
Get on your knees, allow the wood
to splinter your skin as you prise apart
a home filled with moss and periwinkles.
Sing a lament, *Caoineadh na mara* will do,
sketch a dress of loose cotton in sand.
Did you feed it? If so reflect.
Your mother told you, *your mother told you*,
the honey is for you alone.
You let yourself go hungry,
stole the sweetest plums, listened
to his cries of pleasure, stole more.
Remember the feral cat your father
put in the car, the scratches on his skin?
How he drove fifteen miles to be sure.
Remember how she tore into the night,
her yellow eyes never once looked back?
Do that.

Working in Galway

Jack Stewart

I came here to write but have only
Patches of sunlight and the soot
Of pencil erasures on the table
To show for it.
A fly is disappointed
And swerves its way to the window.
If I looked outside, I would not see
Even a recognized absence, just
Some chimneys in need of repair
And probably a few black-headed gulls.
I wish I could say they are
Emblematic of something,
Like friendship or vision.
The monks on this coast
Used the barbed holly-hedge
Of Gothic script for the unknowable.
I have bad handwriting and a need
To say something I don't understand.
The garbage truck that will turn
Into the alley says everything
Lasts. The chimney says nothing
Is wasted.

Every word might be a greeting,
Every word wants you to breathe.
And the white wings that soar
Beyond the horizon
Of this neighbourhood will return.

Phillies

Ling Yuan

'Greenwich Avenue where two streets meet.' – Edward Hopper

1

The restaurant is located in a way
to conceal the fact it exists. Sometimes
people drift here in the dark, not quite sure
which direction to turn, and are surprised
to find Phillies, brightly lit.

2

I was at Phillies once. The day my wife left,
with her clothes, her shoes, her coffee mug
and my potted plant. On the refrigerator,
a note said: *I'm not coming back.*
Just like that. No number. No address.
Except a house too hushed, too hollow.

I went outside but everywhere was
steeped in shadows and stagnant air.
Only the thin crescent moon scowled at me.
Hours, I roamed the streets like a stray ghost,
until leaking around one corner, a whitish
otherworldly light beckoned, morphed itself –

as I drew closer – into a diner. (Enclosed:
one waiter, stooped behind the counter,
and two customers wearing faraway faces.)

Stepping in, I was offered a seat
and hot coffee. But in my mug floated
a loathsome man. Hard as I tried,
I couldn't sweep him aside with the teaspoon.
The waiter shrugged. *That's how it is.*
But why, what do you mean, that's how it is?
She could have told me what went wrong,

she didn't have to leave.

Will

Niamh Twomey

My knapweed brush, evening primrose, speedwell;
I leave them to the bees
who gifted me honey, always sweetened the garden.

The willow that springs along the bank outside my window
I leave to the birds
whose symphony roused me each morning.

My bookshelves, snug with worlds,
I leave to my mother
who was this world's curator.

The woods that hold wisdom like ground-elder
I leave to foxes and badgers
that they may find shelter in pulsing roots.

The field of clover, bird's-foot trefoil and dandelions
I leave to wild horses
to charge down the hillside with the heather.

My house with its whitewashed sills, wooden frames,
this I leave to moss and lichen
to make of it a palace, welcome ferns as footmen by the door.

Plant poems at my graveside –
no oasis made of foam, like golden-saxifrage
I will find all I need in the damp soil, the pealing river.

The Crannóg Questionnaire

Pete Mullineaux

How would you introduce yourself as a writer to those who may not know you?
Poetry was and is my first love – I've published five collections – followed closely by drama. An early stageplay, 'Wallflowers', was produced on the London fringe and since coming to live in Galway I've written a number of plays for youth theatre and for RTÉ radio. I also write songs and was in a punk band in London, before going solo for a while as 'Pete Zero' singer-songwriter. Music and poetry still overlap: my third poetry collection, *Session*, focused on Irish traditional music (Salmon, 2011). In 2021 I finally had a go at fiction with a self-published debut novel, *Jules & Rom – Sci-fi Meets Shakespeare* (Matador), which focuses on AI and emotional intelligence, and offers a new take on one of the most popular plays of all time. Regarding my overall work, I'd say I try to explore ideas in a serious, personal-political way and with what has often been described as quirky and slant humour.

When did you start writing?
I remember making up a song when I was about 6, home in bed with a stomach upset, it went something like, 'I've got a pain in my tummy … oh doc come quick, I'm sick …' The second verse was about a hot water-bottle. My first 'protest song'! My writing received a boost aged 13 when a poem in the school magazine was picked up for an anthology (*Poetry & Song*) by Macmillan & then recorded on Argo Records with music by Ewan McColl & Peggy Seeger.

Do you have a writing routine?
No. Usually ideas, images, feelings come to me when I'm out walking or doing something routine about the house – I let them percolate and when I think they're ready I sit down and write them out.

When you write, do you picture somehow a potential audience or do you just write?
Audiences are not really a factor at the beginning – I mostly enjoy playing around with an idea or image for its own sake, sometimes consciously but often unconscious of what it is I'm trying to work through. Once I've reached a certain stage, I might start thinking of an imaginary listener: how the poem sounds read aloud – the tone, phrasing, rhythm, its overall structure – all of which will impact on re-writes.

Some writers describe themselves as planners, while others plunge right in to the writing. Would you consider yourself a planner or a plunger?
A plunger, I wouldn't think of the gestating period as planning, more a sort of preparing. With the novel I jumped right in with a first draft, which got the story written, but then I had to do a lot of retrospective planning in subsequent re-writes to fix structural issues, plot and character development, etc.

Tell us a bit about your non-literary work experience, please.
I teach Global Citizenship in schools through creative writing – again, mostly through poetry or drama. I work closely with Afri (Action from Ireland) on their Worldwise Global Schools programme as well as Poetry Ireland's Development Education through Literature scheme. I've published several teaching resources, most recently *Interdependence Day: Teaching the Sustainable Development Goals through Drama for All Ages* (Afri, 2021). Way back, I worked as a bus conductor, van driver, community printer, adventure playground worker, secondary school teacher.

What do you like to read in your free time?
A mix of novels, poetry, plays, as well as non-fiction, especially with science, history or environmental themes. I love Mary Oliver's poetry, more recently Colette Bryce, and frequently return to old favourites like Robert Frost. I enjoyed Merlin Sheldrake's *Entangled Life*, Joe O'Connor's novel *Shadowplay* centred on Bram Stoker's association

with the actor/director Henry Irving and actress Ellen Terry in the London theatre; *William Blake versus the World* by John Higgs. I'm fond of sci-fi that's character based and not too techie (Ursula Le Guin, Isaac Asimov, Philip K Dick).

What one book do you wish you had written?
Frankenstein: Mary Shelley wrote such an amazing novel, for all times – the idea of a person made out of bits (of other people) searching for a sense of self, authenticity, identity, security – is such an eternal theme as well as being an amazing metaphor/allegory for our current times. It's considered to be the first sci-fi novel. I like it too that she wrote it from a challenge from her 'writers group' (!) that just happened to include Percy Shelley and Byron.

Do you think writers have a social role to play in society or is their role solely artistic?
Early influences on me were Guthrie and Dylan, novels by Baldwin, Steinbeck, Cordell's books about Welsh mining communities – so from a young age I wanted to be a rebel and change the world. This led into protest songs as well as the kind of poetry I wrote while part of the 'alternative' London performance scene. At one point I recorded an anti-nuclear song, 'Disposable Tissues', as a single. I don't think it can ever be purely artistic: no matter the intention of the writer, simply by producing work and sharing it through publishing and public readings, we're engaged in social interaction and thereby playing a role – saying something in response to the world, potentially influencing others.

Tell us something about your latest publication, please.
We Are the Walrus is my most recent publication (Salmon Poetry, 2022). The poems explore human interaction with nature and ask questions about human nature. I was very happy when the World Wildlife Fund featured it on the cover of their Arctic magazine, *The Circle* – then tweeted it on World Walrus Day! My love for music, especially Irish trad, is reflected in one section of the poems included.

Can writing be taught?
I think the craft can be taught, but it has to go alongside reading and taking in good examples of how words work on the eye and ear. Everyone has something to say and I'd encourage anyone to follow that urge to get what is inside themselves out into the world, turn private into public.

Have you given or attended creative writing workshops and if you have, share your experiences a bit, please.
Both: I've attended and facilitated workshops. I've been hosting a writers group in Oughterard for years, and have also given workshops for literary festivals, libraries, schools and community groups. I enjoy facilitating: meeting new writers, hearing their work, appreciating the personal and often challenging journey some have to make even to attend a workshop. There are actually two poems in *We Are the Walrus* about facilitating – 'Poetry Visit' and 'Don't Always Expect Fireworks' – both based on experience.

Finally, what question do you wish that someone would ask about your writing, and how would you answer it?
I think most writers enjoy (are desperate for!) feedback. It's lovely when someone offers a response to all that hard graft and devotion to something that might have taken years gestating and writing. So a question like: 'I'd like to know more about what you were saying in that poem, in that line, or that part of the novel', would be a real opener. Then part of my answer would include asking what the poem or line said to *them* – so this becomes a conversation. Writers want to connect: one of the reasons we do it in the first place and why we enjoy reading and sharing our work with an audience whenever possible.

Artist's Statement

Cover image: *Space Disco Starling* by Graeme Patterson

Combining sculpture, scale models, stop-motion animation, robotics, interactive programming, virtual reality and music, Graeme Patterson's work plunges us into a world that is as moving as it is playful. The product of a slow and meticulous creative process, his work entices us into an emotionally-charged parallel universe inhabited by dreams, games, memory and nostalgia.

His work has been exhibited at museums and galleries internationally. He has also screened his animated films at several international festivals including the Toronto International Film Festival and the Reykjavik International Film Festival.

Space Disco Starling is from a unique installation entitled *Strange Birds* commenting on climate change. Habitats are being destroyed, disasters happening and new species taking over from those who have always lived in their natural environments. The starling features in this work of art make reference to a colonial history within the region which has impacted native birds such as the blue heron.
http://www.graemepatterson.com

Biographical Details

Peter Adair's poems have appeared in *Poetry Ireland Review*, *The Honest Ulsterman*, *Abridged*, *Howl* and many other journals. He is a recipient of an Arts Council bursary through the Support for Individual Artists Programme.

Liam Aungier has had poems published in *The Irish Times*, *Poetry Ireland Review*, *Cyphers*, and previously in *Crannóg*. A collection, *Apples in Winter*, was published by Doghouse.

Ivy Bannister has published a poetry collection, *Vinegar and Spit*, a memoir, *Blunt Trauma*, and a collection of short stories, *Magician*. Her awards include a Hennessy award and the Francis MacManus award. Recent work has appeared in *Tearing Stripes off Zebras* and *Well, You Don't Look It*.

Gerard Beirne has published three collections of poetry, most recently *The Death Poems*, (Salt Publishing, 2024). He has also published four novels and a collection of short stories. He lectures on the BA Writing and Literature Programme at ATU Sligo.

Laura Treacy Bentley is a poet, novelist, and point-and-shoot photographer from West Virginia. She has been published in the United States and Ireland in *Poetry Ireland Review*, *The Stinging Fly*, *Crannóg*, *The New York Quarterly*, *Poetry Daily*, and *O Magazine*, among others. Work is forthcoming in *We Are Appalachia!* and in *Goldenseal*. She is the author of *The Silver Tattoo*, a psychological thriller; *Lake Effect*, a poetry collection; *Night Terrors*, a short story prequel to *The Silver Tattoo*; *Looking for Ireland: An Irish-Appalachian Pilgrimage*, a poetry and photography chapbook; and a picture book, *Sir Grace and the Big Blizzard*.

Peter Branson is a poet, songwriter and singer whose poetry has been published widely, including in *Acumen*, *Agenda*, *Ambit*, *Envoi*, *The London Magazine*, *The North*, *Prole*, *The Warwick Review*, *Iota*, *The Frogmore Papers* and others. *Red Hill, Selected Poems* was published in 2013 by Lapwing, Belfast. *Hawk Rising*, also from Lapwing, was published in 2016. He was highly commended in the Petra Kenny International Poetry Prize and won first prizes in the Grace Dieu and the Envoi International competitions. He was first-prize winner in the 2019/21 Sentinel Poetry Book Competition for *Marrowbones* which was published in 2021 and he won first prize in the Littoral Poetry Book Competition 2020/21 for *The Clear Daylight* also published in 2021.

Lauren Camp currently serves as New Mexico Poet Laureate. She is the author of eight books of poetry, most recently *In Old Sky* (Grand Canyon Conservancy, 2024). She is a recipient of the Dorset Prize, honourable mention for the Arab American Book Award and Adrienne Rich Award, and fellowships from the Academy of American Poets and Black Earth Institute. Her poems have been translated into Mandarin, Turkish, Spanish, French and Arabic. She is a former Astronomer-in-Residence at Grand Canyon National Park. www.laurencamp.com

Sean Coffey has twice been shortlisted for the Francis MacManus Prize, also for the Hennessy Prize, the Sean O'Faolain Short Story Prize, the Anthology Short Story Prize, the Fish Short Story Prize, and his fiction appears in a number of publications.

Louise G Cole won a Hennessy Award in 2018. Carol Ann Duffy chose her pamphlet *Soft Touch* for publication in the final Laureate's Choice series. She has had poetry pamphlets commended in Munster Literature Centre's annual Fool for Poetry Competition on three occasions. *Under the Influence* was published by Hedgehog Poetry Press in 2022. www.louisegcolewriter.com.

Rachael Davey's poems have been published in *Rialto, Strix, New Welsh Review* and elsewhere. She currently works on a wetland nature reserve.

Maurice Devitt is a past winner of the Trócaire/Poetry Ireland and Poems for Patience competitions. He published his debut collection *Growing Up in Colour* with Doire Press in 2018. He is curator of the Irish Centre for Poetry Studies site. His Pushcart-nominated poem 'The Lion Tamer Dreams of Office Work' was the title poem of an anthology published by Hibernian Writers in 2015. His second collection, *Some of These Stories Are True*, was published by Doire Press in 2023.

Maitreyabandhu Dharmachari is a Buddhist teacher, poet, critic and writer. He has published three poetry pamphlets and three full-length collections with Bloodaxe Books: *The Crumb Road* (2013), a PBS Recommendation, *Yarn* (2015), and *After Cézanne* (2019), a sequence of 56 poems about the life of the painter. He was ordained into the Triratna Buddhist Order in 1990 and lives and works at the London Buddhist Centre.

Deborah H. Doolittle is an AWP Intro Award winner and Pushcart Prize nominee. She is the author of *Floribunda* and three chapbooks, *No Crazy Notions, That Echo,* and *Bogbound*.

Daragh Fleming's debut in non-fiction, *Lonely Boy*, was published by BookHub Publishing. He has work appearing in several literary magazines including *The Ogham Stone, Gutter Magazine, Ropes, Beir Bua, Trasna, The Madrigal* and others. Recently he was shortlisted for the Alpine Fellowship Poetry Prize and highly commended for both the Patrick Kavanagh Award and the Fool For Poetry Prize and long-listed for The London Magazine Poetry Prize.

Nicola Geddes is a multi-disciplinary artist: poet, musician, visual artist and teacher. She studied Environmental Art at the Glasgow School of Art and holds a Diploma in Cello Performance from the London College of Music. She has been published in *The Irish Times, Poetry Ireland Review, Crannóg, The Galway Review, Crossways, The Blue Nib, Skylight 47* and *Poethead,* and internationally on the *Extinction Rebellion Global Creative* online hub, in the *Pinch* journal (USA) and *The National* (Scotland). Her poems have been broadcast on Lyric fm in Ireland and on Swiss national television, and can be found in the anthologies *Writing Home* (Dedalus Press) and *Children of the Nation* (Culture Matters), *Tell Me Who We Were Before Life Made Us* (3 of Cups Press), *Workers Write!* (Blue Cubicle Press) and

Poems for When you Can't Find the Words (Irish Hospice Foundation/Poetry Ireland). She received Special Commendation in the Patrick Kavanagh Award in 2017, and was Highly Commended in 2018 in the Over the Edge New Writer of the Year. In May 2019 she won *The Irish Times*' New Irish Writing.

Rebecca Gethin has published five poetry books and two novels. She was a Hawthornden Fellow and a Poetry School tutor. Her poems are widely published in various magazines and anthologies. She won the first Coast to Coast pamphlet competition with *Messages*. Her pamphlet *Snowlines* has recently been published by Maytree Press. www.rebeccagethin.wordpress.com.

Mark Granier's fifth poetry collection, *Ghostlight: New & Selected Poems*, was published by Salmon in 2017. His sixth is forthcoming in 2025.

Aideen Henry has been published in *The Irish Times*, *The Stinging Fly* and broadcast on RTÉ Radio 1. She was shortlisted for the Hennessy XO Literary Award, the Francis MacManus Award and received a Literature Bursary Award from the Irish Arts Council. Her two collections of poetry, *Hands Moving at the Speed of Falling Snow* and *Slow Bruise*, were published with Salmon Poetry. Her collection of short stories, *Hugging Thistles*, was published by Arlen House.

Margaret Hickey worked in London for many years, notably as editor of *Departures*, a London-based literary travel magazine, and as an editor at *Country Living* magazine. She also contributed articles to several newspapers including *The Financial Times*, *The Guardian* and *The Times*. Her first book, *Irish Days*, a collection of oral histories, was published in 2001 and her most recent book, *Ireland's Green Larder*, is a history of Ireland seen through the prism of food and drink.

Bob Hicok is the author of *Water Look Away* (Copper Canyon Press, 2023). He has received a Guggenheim and two NEA Fellowships, the Bobbitt Prize from the Library of Congress, nine Pushcart Prizes, and was twice a finalist for the National Book Critics Circle Award. His poems have appeared in *Poetry*, *The New Yorker*, *The Paris Review*, and nine volumes of *The Best American Poetry*.

Maryellen Hodgins has been published in *Crannóg*, *Revival Poetry*, *Cyphers*, *THE SHOp*, *Live Encounters*, and *The Galway Review*. She has published two collections of poetry: *Driftwood* with Revival Press and *Life Poems* with Tribes Press.

Fred Johnston (1951-2024) was an Irish poet, novelist, literary critic and musician. He was the founder of the Western Writers' Centre in Galway, *Ionad Scríbhneoiri Chaitlín Maude*. Together with Neil Jordan and Peter Sheridan he co-founded the Irish Writers' Co-operative in 1974, and founded Galway's annual Cúirt International Festival of Literature in 1986. He published ten collections of poetry, three novels, and three short story collections. He reviewed poetry for *Poetry Ireland Review*, *Books Ireland*, the *Southern Humanities Review*, *The Irish Times* and *Harpers & Queen*, and contributed to the literary magazines *Orbis*, *New Letters*, *The Southern Review*, *The Seneca Review*, *Irish Studies Review* and others. He received the Prix de l'Ambassade Translation bursary to work on translations of the French poet Michel

Martin. He has also translated the Senegalese poet Babacar Sall, and the Breton poet Colette Wittorski, and also received The Ireland Fund of Monaco bursary to be writer-in-residence for a month at the Princess Grace Irish Library in Monaco. With his folk group Parson's Hat he released two albums, *Cutty Wren* and *The Better Match*.

Breda Joyce's poetry has won and been shortlisted for awards, most recently the inaugural Yeats Thoor Ballylee award. Her poems have appeared in *The Irish Times*, *Poems from Pandemia*, *Crannóg*, *Skylight 47*, *The Honest Ulsterman*, *The Galway Review*, *Best of British and Irish Poets*, *The Waxed Lemon* and others. Her essays have been broadcast on RTÉ's *Sunday Miscellany*. Her first collection *Reshaping the Light* was published by Chaffinch Press in 2021.

Hugo Kelly has won many awards for his short fiction including the Cúirt New Writing Award and the Maria Edgeworth Short Story Competition. He has twice been shortlisted for the New Irish Writing Award for Emerging Fiction and the RTÉ Francis MacManus Award. His short stories have appeared previously in *Crannóg* and *the Stinging Fly* and have been broadcast on BBC Radio 4 and RTÉ Radio 1. In 2023 he was awarded a mentorship by the National Mentoring Writing Programme. He is a librarian at the University of Galway.

Claire-Lise Kieffer's poetry has been published in the Dedalus Press *Local Wonders* and *Romance Options* anthologies, in *Skylight 47*, *The Waxed Lemon*, *The Madrigal*, *Poethead*, *Abridged*, *Beir Bua* and more. She was shortlisted for the 2021 Fish Poetry Prize and was highly commended in the Cúirt New Writing Prize in 2024. Her flash fiction was a winner in the 2022 Books Ireland competition.

Brian Kirk has published two collections with Salmon Poetry, *After The Fall* (2017) and *Hare's Breath* (2023) and a fiction chapbook with Southword Editions *It's Not Me It's You* (2019). His novel *Riverrun* was a winner of the Irish Writers' Centre Novel Fair in 2022.

Robert Leach is a member of the Scottish Book Trust's Live Literature panel. He has been Chair of the Borders Writers Forum and President of the Melrose Literary Society. His published work includes biographies, travel books and books of theatre history and theatre theory. His *Theatre Workshop: Joan Littlewood and the Making of Modern British Theatre* (Exeter University Press, 2006) and his two-volume *Illustrated History of British Theatre and Performance* (Routledge, 2019) were both shortlisted for Theatre Book of the Year. He has held senior posts at Birmingham and Edinburgh Universities – and is also a theatre director. His production of *I Want a Baby* by Sergei Tretyakov remained in the repertoire of the Teatr u Nikitskih Vorot in Moscow for five years.

V.P. Loggins is the author of *The Wild Severance* (2021), winner of the 26th Annual Bright Hill Press Poetry Book Competition, *The Green Cup* (2017), winner of the *Cider Press Review* Editors' Book Prize, *The Fourth Paradise* (Editor's Select Poetry Series, Main Street Rag, 2010), and *Heaven Changes* (Pudding House Chapbook Series 2007). He has also published a book on Shakespeare, *The Life of Our Design*, and is co-author of another, *Shakespeare's Deliberate Art*. His poems have appeared in *The Baltimore Review*, *English Journal*, *Poet Lore*, *Poetry East*, *Poetry Ireland Review*, *The Southern Review* and *Tampa Review*, and others. www.vploggins.com.

Laurence Lumsden has previously been published in *Sky Island Journal*, *The River*, and *The Galway Review*.

David Lynch is an award-winning journalist who has published three books of non-fiction, the most recent being *Confronting Shadows: An Introduction to the Poetry of Thomas Kinsella* (New Island, 2015). In 2022 he was awarded an Arts Council Agility Award for his short story work.

Noelle Lynskey completed her MA in Creative Writing in UL and Strokestown's Poet Laureate in 2021. She has had work broadcast on RTÉ's *Sunday Miscellany* and published in *The Irish Times*, and in anthologies and journals including *Staying Human*, *Washing Windows*, *Crannóg*, *Romance Options*, *Drawn to the Light* and *Local Wonders*. She facilitates Portumna Pen Pushers and is advisor to Shorelines Arts Festival.

Aoibheann McCann is a writer and performer. Her first novel, *Marina*, was published in 2018. Her work has been anthologised by New Binary Press, Arlen House, Prospero (IT), Doire Press and others. Her short stories have appeared in literary magazines including *The Stinging Fly* and previously in *Crannóg*. She co-writes, produces, directs and acts in the chart-topping audio comedy *Retreat*.

Karen J McDonnell's poetry and other writing has been published widely at home and in the US, UK and Australia. Her poems have won awards and appeared on several shortlists, including Poem of the Year at the An Post Irish Book Awards. She has read her work at many festivals and on RTÉ Radio's *Lyric Poem*, *Sunday Miscellany*, *Arena*, and *The Poetry Programme*. Her debut poetry collection *This Little World* is published by Doire Press. She is currently working on her second collection. Karenjmcdonnell.com

Kate McHugh has been published in *ROPES*, *Southword*, and *Drawn to the Light Press*.

Katie McIvor's short fiction has appeared or is forthcoming in magazines such as *The Deadlands*, *PodCastle*, and *Little Blue Marble*, and her three-story collection is out now with Ram Eye Press. @McKatie_ katiemcivor.com.

Alan McMonagle has written for radio and published two collections of short stories, *Psychotic Episodes* and *Liar Liar*. His first novel, *Ithaca*, was published by Picador in 2017 and was longlisted for the Desmond Elliott Award for first novels, the Dublin Literary Award, and shortlisted for an Irish Book Award. His second novel, *Laura Cassidy's Walk Of Fame*, appeared in 2020.

Kathleen Magher's stories have been previously published in *Crannóg*, in various literary journals in Canada, and anthologised in *Outskirts: Women Writing From Small Places*.

James Martyn Joyce writes short stories and poetry.

Nicole Morris is a poet and essayist. Her poetry has been published in *Glass Poetry* and *Banshee*. She was a non-fiction finalist in the 2024 Disquiet International Literary Prize and will attend the Disquiet International residency in Lisbon, followed by the Roots. Wounds. Words. Retreat for Storytellers of Color in autumn. She is completing an MA in Creative Writing at the University of Galway.

John Reinhart is a recipient of the Horror Writers Association Dark Poetry Scholarship and a member of the Science Fiction and Fantasy Poetry Association. He is the author of nine collections of poetry. http://home.hampshire.edu/~jcr00/reinhart.html.

Lorna Shaughnessy is a poet, translator and researcher. She has published five poetry collections, most recently *Lark Water* (Salmon Poetry, 2021). She has translated four volumes of Mexican and Spanish poetry and co-edited *A Different Eden: Ecopoetry from Ireland and Galicia* (Dedalus, 2021). https://lornashaughnessy.com/

Jo Slade is a poet and artist. Her most recent poetry collection is *Cycles and Lost Monkeys* (Salmon Poetry, 2019). A new collection, *O N C E*, is due out from Salmon Poetry in 2024.

Breda Spaight's debut collection *Watching for the Hawk* was shortlisted for the Farmgate Café National Poetry Prize in 2024. Her poem 'The Curse' was a finalist in the Forward Prize Best Single Poem Written 2023.

Bobbie Sparrow recently published her debut poetry collection *The Weight of Blood* with Yaffle Press. She is a widely published poet with poems in journals and anthologies and her work has been placed in several well-known competitions.

Jack Stewart was educated at the University of Alabama and Emory University and was a Brittain Fellow at The Georgia Institute of Technology. His first book, *No Reason*, was published by the Poeima Poetry Series in 2020, and his work has appeared in numerous journals and anthologies, including *Poetry*, *The American Literary Review*, *A New Ulster*, *Image*, and others. He currently runs the Talented Writers Program at Pine Crest School in Fort Lauderdale, Florida.

Niamh Twomey won the 2023 Desmond O'Grady International Poetry Competition and the 2022 Trim Poetry Competition. Her work has appeared in journals and anthologies such as *The London Magazine*, *Rattle*, and *Banshee*, among others. She is currently undertaking a PhD at Queen's University Belfast.

Ling Yuan is a Business graduate of Nanyang Technological University and has previously attended fiction workshops at Asia Creative Writing Programme.

Stay in touch with
Crannóg
@
www.crannogmagazine.com

Milton Keynes UK
Ingram Content Group UK Ltd.
UKHW051953291024
450259UK00004B/12